ELECTRO-MAGNETIC PULSE
(L A T E N T   L U N A T I C S)

ELECTRO-MAGNETIC PULSE
(L A T E N T   L U N A T I C S)

Ronald E. Runge

Writers Club Press
New York   Bloomington

Writers Club Press: an imprint of iUniverse, Inc.

iUniverse books may be ordered through booksellers or by contacting:

iUniverse
1663 Liberty Drive
Bloomington, IN 47403
www.iuniverse.com
1-800-Authors (1-800-288-4677)

Because of the dynamic nature of the Internet, any Web addresses or links contained in this book may have changed since publication and may no longer be valid. The views expressed in this work are solely those of the author and do not necessarily reflect the views of the publisher, and the publisher hereby disclaims any responsibility for them.

ISBN: 978-1-4401-5652-6 (sc)
ISBN: 978-1-4401-5653-3 (ebook)

Printed in the United States of America

iUniverse rev. date: 08/24/2009

CONTENTS

CHAPTER I
REVIEW EXPERT

Air Force Captain Kurt Reitz leaned back in his extra comfortable, all around chair. The last six hours had he had kept his never moving eyes glued on the several computer screens which decked his otherwise empty, spacious desk. These screens were as important as any to be found in the United States of America.

The Captain, still leaning, had earned a well deserved half hour of eye and back rest, before finishing the remaining two hours of his usual, eight hours a day, five days a week, sometimes including weekends, tour of official duty, as a "Systems Review Expert".

Captain Reitz's office, this twentieth day of March, 2005, looked like any other office with a set of computer banks, except this office happened to be in the middle of a mountain. The Rocky Mountains, near Colorado Springs, Colorado, to be exact. This was America's prestigious, first rate, Cheyenne Mountain "Operations Center". The Center was an integral part of, and associated with the Nuclear Defense group known as the "North American Aerospace Defense Command", also known as "NORAD".

The Air Force had won the decision to build the massive bunker inside Cheyenne Mountain back in 1959, when the nation heartily agreed that this most important American defense necessity had to be nuclear bomb safe.

In 1960, the Army Corp of Engineers was commissioned to supervise the building of the complex, which included excavating enough inner mountain material to construct fifteen separate building size room areas inside the bunker, along with sleeping quarters, a doctor and hospital facility, food cooking and food eating areas, huge water retention tanks, and even a barber shop. The main compound also rested on huge shock absorbing steel springs.

Unique features of the complex are the more than one hundred thousand, thirty-two foot long, implosion preventing bolts, plus a horseshoe shaped tunnel - - - and an ingenious funnel, designed to sweep the main force of a nuclear blast past the bunker's two gigantic twenty-five ton steel blast doors.

The mountain bunker had been completed by 1966, complete with barbed wire, and machine gun emplacements, surrounding the outside perimeter, along with a prohibiting fence, all to keep any saboteurs away.

Four of the mountain bunker's rooms were dedicated solely to the housing, and the manning of the highly complicated and complex computer systems, which were used by the captains to become aware of, to follow and then to identify any and all missile launches from anywhere in the world, which could possibly become a nuclear attack on America.

The several Air Force officers operating the system, all computer experts, were like Captain Kurt Reitz, given extensive training in understanding the system, even beyond their expertise. It would require several months of on-the-job training, along with on-the-job supervision during the last two months, all of which Captain Reitz was now undergoing.

The review officers also were required to absorb twelve study guides, and to master nine hundred critical computer tasks, and then to pass a rigorous final test, before being approved.

Captain Kurt Reitz had not always been such an expert. In fact, he had not been a captain for very long. During several prior years, he had labored as an Aerospace Engineer, for Bowing Aircraft, at their corporate headquarters in Seattle, Washington. He worked as part of their design section.

Kurt earlier had graduated from the Engineering School, at Iowa State University, in Ames, Iowa, in 1995, and he was awarded a degree in Aerospace Engineering. Upon graduation, he was quickly signed up by people from the Bowing Corporation.

From 1995, to February, 2003, Kurt labored daily, weekly, monthly, and yearly on aircraft design options given him by the Bowing hierarchy. These dealt mostly with various aspects of cargo aircraft, including the Air Force tankers, and similar commercial passenger planes.

Kurt, who, while at the engineering school in Ames, became a self-instructed, early expert on the then semi-primitive, existing university computers. He was, however, able to use them to quickly and accurately solve the many aircraft design problems asked for by his engineering professors, usually way in advance of his fellow students, some of whom were still using slide rules. This led to Kurt's top grades, and also to the top recommendations given by his professors.

While at Bowing, Kurt was able to use the more complex computers available there, to a level also, since 2000, he had not experienced at Ames. Still they were not what he wanted, or what Kurt was capable of understanding.

On his own, Kurt purchased from a new computer company, Microsoft, also in Washington State, highly advanced, parts of extraordinary functioning computer sections, all miniaturized. He was able to assemble the same into a highly operational computer system, far in advance of anything used at work.

Kurt was able to put his computer contraptions together at his apartment in Seattle, often spending hours on his homemade computer, after the workday at Bowing, and doing interesting design work they would not let him do at the aircraft company.

His interests lay in putting together the total design of all aspects of an all purpose fighter plane, which Kurt felt would have an operational ability above and beyond the fighter planes then in operation in the American Air Force, or even on the drawing boards.

In January of 2003, Kurt was instructed by the Bowing hierarchy to contact an Air Force captain, John Jackson, who was one of Bowing's Air Force test pilots. Jackson was to inform Kurt about his impressions of a flying test he had made a week earlier on certain aspects of the tanker design Bowing was pushing, and that Kurt was working on.

Jackson's air design knowledge, and flying ability, impressed Kurt. Kurt's design ability, along with his superior computer knowledge and use, impressed Jackson. The two, as such, got along just like two peas in a pod.

During those few days that Kurt and John had worked together, John also became aware that Kurt had completed some early fighter designs on his self-built, home computer, and John quickly realized, after scanning the designs, of their superior concepts. He also became highly interested in Kurt's unique home computer. On the last day of their Bowing work, John asked to see it.

The two, now fast friends, had such common mutual interests, that Kurt readily assented, taking John to his apartment that night to show off his special computer.

Kurt, immediately after the computer was given power, exhibited its extraordinary, superior qualities, which John, amazed, readily admitted.

He told Kurt, "You are one Engineer in a million. I would have bet a trillion dollars that a single person could not have been able to put together this highly advanced computer system," adding, "The only other place I have seen such an equal in computers is at the North American Aerospace Defense Command inside Cheyenne Mountain."

"What is that?" asked Kurt.

"The Force command center that is responsible for defending America against any nuclear attack," John replied. "Wow, would they love to have an expert like you."

Kurt, now very interested, kept questioning John about the computer setup at Cheyenne Mountain. When John told Kurt that it could be very likely, should Kurt make the necessary application, and John also gave the Air Force his glowing recommendation, that the Air Force would automatically, taking into account Kurt's aerospace experience, and his university degree, grant him a captain's commission, and then assign him to duty at Cheyenne Mountain for the entire term of his four year enlistment.

Kurt, salivating for an opportunity to get his hands on such advanced computers, told John, "I would be very interested in becoming part of Cheyenne Mountain. In fact," Kurt added, "I would voluntarily do whatever the Air Force wanted, if I knew I could be commissioned a captain, and then be given a guarantee to remain at the Cheyenne Mountain computers during any agreed tour of duty."

John, as he left the apartment told Kurt, "I have to be there for a mission in ten days. I will make it a point to talk to them and let you know."

By January 30, 2005, John had made the necessary Air Force arrangements. By February 15, 2005, Kurt had been notified he would be commissioned a captain, and then be assigned to Cheyenne Mountain. By February 23, 2005, Kurt had submitted the necessary resignations to Bowing, and on March 1, 2005, Captain Kurt Reitz took his officer's oath, and began his tour of duty in front of those absolutely gorgeous computers as a trainee with the eventual designation as a Systems Review Expert.

Kurt sat down the piping hot, welcome, cup of coffee, as he and his supervisor, an Air Force major, went over the relevant computer readings of the last six hours. The Major purposely interrogating Kurt on various aspects, testing him, here and there, in an effort to confound him.

At the conclusion of their coffee get together in the captain's mess, the Major smiled, and slapping Kurt on the back, said, "Excellent job Captain, you are the best of any of my students."

As Kurt and the Major made their way back to the command computers, Kurt told him, "This has got to be the most secure nuclear defense facility in the world. In just the short time I have been here, we have fully identified many missile launches, using only the heat they generate. Our computers, and auxiliary equipment, have to be the best."

"America has to be proud of Cheyenne Mountain," the Major agreed, adding, "As a matter of fact, the Pentagon is developing plans to build an additional command center right here in our mountain."

"What is that all about?" asked Kurt. "Is that something new?"

"US Northern Command is a new military district put together as the aftermath of the New York Towers attack of September 11, 2001," the Major responded. "Admiral Timothy Keating is the commander of Northern," adding, "It is presently located at Peterson Air Force Base, which is a little on the other side of Colorado Springs, about twenty-five minutes' drive from here."

"Will Northern be able to use the same facilities here at the mountain, as NORAD?" Kurt inquired.

"Keating was here talking to reporters just a few days ago," the Major replied. "The Admiral was really bragging about Cheyenne Mountain, saying, 'He was looking forward to the US Northern Command working alongside NORAD, and that NORAD had so many significant improvements to the operating computer system and the other operations,'" adding, "'And we've got it right here at Cheyenne Mountain. This is state-of-the-art.'"

"That must have happened on my day off," Kurt intoned.

"Keating also talked about opening a new, larger operation center in the mountain," concluded the Major as they arrived at Captain Reitz's bank of computers, and Kurt prepared to work.

Before losing himself in his computers, Kurt commented, "As you know, I'm new to the Air Force. Isn't General Rosann Bailey the Commander of NORAD? How does Admiral Keating get involved?"

"Keating, as Commander of US Northern Command, is the top officer over all military units in the Northern Command sector, which includes Cheyenne Mountain and NORAD."

Kurt nodding his head, "Now I understand. It is part of the Chain-of-Command," adding, "But there is something else I am highly concerned about. I'm confident, our computers, largely by detecting the heat emanating from a nuclear, or any other kind of missile, when it is launched, can accurately pinpoint where and when the missile was sent into the air," adding, "And I'm confident we at NORAD can discover that problem, but can we protect America after we discover it?

"My information is that our actual responding Missile Defense System is plainly primitive," Kurt related. "There has been a critical strategic failure to protect America from such a ballistic missile attack. Bush has had two terms of his presidency to push for an adequate system, the result is still only a limited defense, consisting of a small number of ground based interceptors, with a limited sea-based system, still on the drawing boards."

The Major nodding in agreement, commented, "Our politicians seem to be more concerned about their lobbying friends' concerns, then about the survival of America," adding, "We have known, since 1991, the election period of President Clinton, that the use of space-based interceptors, which can attack enemy nuclear missiles in their ascent stage, is the most effective defense. Tests conducted way back have proven the space-based defense feasible."

Kurt intoned, "I agree," as he adjusted his computers, adding, "As President Reagan, who made sure we were aware of the space-based concept, said, 'If we lose freedom here, there is no place to escape to. This is the last stand on earth.'"

CHAPTER II
JOHN "BLITZ" JACKSON

K urt, still a single man, chose to use the Cheyenne Mountain's sleeping rooms during the times he was on duty. It was easier. He did, however, rent a small apartment in Colorado Springs, for use, on his days and weekends off. While he used the space for extra clothing, gear, and his extensive library, it was mainly to house his growing homemade, complex computer system, which also allowed Kurt to continue work on his fighter design.

John Jackson, now a major, Kurt's Air Force test pilot friend, was at the "Mountain" for official business, and made a point to stop by to see how his friend was doing. He also remained interested in Karl's homemade computer, and his aeronautical designs, asking, "Do you still have that unique computer somewhere? Are you still working on that interesting fighter plane design?" adding, "I've only told two people about it," he laughed, "My wife and my test pilot commander, who I have sworn to secrecy."

Kurt smiled, nodding his head, and interposed, "I've got the whole contraption at an apartment in Colorado Springs. In fact, I've added a few new wrinkles to it," adding, "I've also been working on developing an additional stealth concept to it."

"I would really like to see them," John replied.

"I have this next weekend off," Kurt responded. "If you can make it then, I will be happy to show you my latest endeavors. Besides, I owe you a grand dinner. Actually many more of them, for what you have done for me," adding, chuckling, "But you will also have to swear your wife's secrecy along with the CO."

John laughing, clapped Kurt on his back, saying, "You've got a deal."

John continued, "I have already discussed your 'Mountain' performance with the supervising major. He is extremely satisfied with you. In fact, he calls you, 'his best student.'"

Just at this time, the Major made a surprise appearance, saying, "Blitz, they want to see you at the command office."

Kurt turned his head and intoned, "What did you call him?"

"Blitz, Blitz Jackson," the Major replied. "That's how I have always known him."

As John turned to leave, he said, "I will tell you about it later. I do plan to be at your place Saturday afternoon. Write down the address."

That weekend, March 25, 2005, quickly arrived, and Kurt, like a proud father, displayed his complex computer contraption to Major Jackson, who commented, "I think the stealth concepts, along with a lot of the new wing and tail alignments deserve a mention to the upper Air Force procurement brass."

Kurt flattered, said, "That really helps my ego. I wish you would hold off until I put down some additional ideas and details," adding, "Right now, I want to treat you to an excellent homemade steak and a good wine, from the kitchen of a girlfriend I recently met. She is not only a real looker, and smart, but she can also cook."

"Anybody can broil or charcoal steaks," John intoned, laughing, as they headed out for dinner.

"I must apologize," John admitted later, after a sumptuous dinner, "Those were excellent oven cooked steaks. The sauce made them extra good."

"I hope you like the wine," Kurt commented. "The guy that runs the liquor store says it is the best," chuckling, "It was expensive enough."

"Do you think I was worth it," John laughed, as he pulled out the cork, and poured wine into the three goblets, Kurt's girlfriend had brought in from the kitchen.

"A toast to you, young lady," John said, as they clunked glasses, "Excellent food."

She smiled as she picked up the used plates, saying, "I will leave you two alone, while I clean up in the kitchen."

"That is an ideal woman," John commented, after she left.

Kurt, disregarding the remark, poured new glasses of wine, saying, "Here is to Cheyenne Mountain."

After that toast, Kurt then intoned, "You were going to tell me about how you came to be known as Blitz?"

"Well it's kind of embarrassing," John interposed. "I have told my friends not to call me that, but they insist on it."

John continued, "It all started right after I graduated from flight school, and after getting my wings. I had some additional training, in the A-10 as a brand new lieutenant, I was then assigned to an Air Force base in Germany in 1998. President Clinton, and the European Union, was then conducting their war in Kosovo against the Serbian Christians on behalf of the Albanian, Moslem, drug lords."

John continued, "At the time, I was still flying the old, slow A-10 fighter plane, which, however, was a perfect airplane to interdict ground troops, and to harass armored vehicles. It was also heavily armed," adding, "I, and two other fly mates, because of the A-10's, were sent into the Kosovo fray to, ostensibly, dislodge a group of Serb guerillas."

He continued, "I spotted a group first, and brought in the other two A-10's. We were trying to decide what to do. It was then that we picked up a German NATO unit, which radioed that they were under intense fire from an unknown group. We were able to pickup the transmission on our radios and I knew enough German to see they were in real trouble. At the same time, we spotted some anti-aircraft rocket rounds coming in toward us from near the stranded German unit. I was finally able to spot the source. It appeared to be a group of irregulars with a perfect hiding place at the upper lip of a deep defile, but which also had a perfect panoramic view of the entire area. They were also busy lobbing mortar rounds all around those NATO troops," adding, "One of the anti-aircraft rounds found its mark, and hit one of our slow moving A-10's. It did not shoot him down, but I had to send him back to a nearby air strip."

John continued, "I then told the other A-10 to standby while I made a strafing and missile run. I, luckily, found an opportune opening, which allowed me to come in from near the base of their defile and, aided by my heavy armament that had been loaded on my fighter, I was able to take out the entire attacking unit, including every one of their mortars and anti-aircraft rocket launchers," adding, "The Germans surprised, radioed their thanks, and yelled, into the radio receiver that my strafing run was like, 'a one man Blitz Krieg.' They also admitted they had never seen anything like it," laughing, "The other A-10 pilot picked it up and started calling me Blitz.

"End of story," John concluded.

"Were you able to identify the attacking group?" Kurt asked.

"The German commander later informed the Allied Command, they had identified the group, after my strafing, as an Albanian group, and that they were transporting illegal drugs," John admitted, laughing, adding, "Needless to say, the whole incident was hushed up, after all we can't help the Christians, can we?

"Calling me Blitz took on a life of its own."

After another glass of wine, Kurt asked John, tongue-in-cheek, calling him, "Blitz, tell me what is in store for our Cheyenne Mountain."

"'Et tu,' as Caesar said," Blitz laughed, adding, "But my Air Force bosses view the vast cyberspace as an important fighting domain. American businesses also depend on the Internet. However, the nation, and the Air Force deserve priority, because it is the key to our cross-domain defense doctrine."

Blitz continued, "I'm talking about the speed, range, and flexibility of our air power to be able to deliver satellite guided air strikes on an enemy. This can vitally affect the outcome of a battle on the ground. The reason we can do this, is our cyber dominance, which is the ability to move our control signals through cyberspace," adding, "In fact, the Air Force is now in the process of establishing a new command called 'Cyberspace Command'."

"It sounds like the use of space for business, and also for the military, which could lead to a conflict of interests," Kurt interposed. "The national defense should have the priority on the use of the satellites."

"My Air Force bosses are also in conflict about that," Blitz responded.

"The Congress should set our official policies and priorities, with the military being dominant in cyberspace," adding, "Even now China and Russia present a missile challenge, as America has been lagging in engaging the cyberspace battle."

"What do you mean?" asked Kurt.

"Both Russia and China will, of course, do what is in their best interests," Blitz replied. "Maybe this might coincide with American interests, but, maybe not. Russia is presently modernizing, and has already developed a new ballistic missile. This is a new type of hypersonic vehicle. Their testing has also proven its ability to maneuver in orbit so it can easily dodge any present missile we might send up to destroy it. We do have the technology to neutralize these new types of missiles, but they are still on the drawing boards."

"What about China?" Kurt intoned.

"Ah, there is the rub," Blitz responded. "Since Clinton gave away all of America's nuclear technology, missile designs, and other critical military secrets to China, we have a real problem," adding, "As we know, China has two million men in its military. They now possess a bunch of short range missiles, mostly aimed at Taiwan. The thing that should concern America the most is that they now possess thirty to fifty intercontinental ballistic missiles, all aimed at the US. China is building its arsenal by one missile per every couple weeks."

Blitz continued, "China's belligerent attitude, which should even concern liberals, who are dead set against missile defense, is openly and stridently anti-American. Its military writes, and talks, candidly about using their military might on four different fronts, the economic, nuclear, terrorist, and finally, in cyberspace, against us," adding, "In cyberspace, they are investing heavily in missile launch vehicles, and in extensive anti-satellite weaponry, aimed at taking down America's satellites."

"Are we not updating our cyberspace defenses?" Kurt asked. "We evidently know how."

"The liberals right now," Blitz replied, "say they are depending on the old Carter-Bush I doctrine of 'Mutual Assured Destruction', but the present state of our missile defense is extremely limited, and will not protect us."

"I don't understand," Kurt admitted. "If we know what communist

China is doing, and we know how to counteract it, why aren't we doing it?"

"The reason Bush II and the liberals give," Blitz disclosed, "is that we must first win the so-called Middle East War on terror, and in that, they think we need China's help,"

Kurt shook his head in disbelief, commenting, "How can the liberals play this way with the lives and the future of the American people? Somehow that attitude has to change."

Kurt continued, "You mentioned that we have the ability to actually mount a missile defense. What is it?"

"We must first," Blitz replied, "Expand our land based Missile Defense System. Right now it only extends to Alaska and California," adding, "We also have an AEGIS System on our Navy ships, but that is also limited."

Blitz continued, "What we need in cyberspace is the old concept of space based interceptors, hovering out in space. They can quickly respond to any enemy's missile launch, and would be able to destroy the missile, and blow up its warhead in its ascent stage."

"Is that what they called the 'Pebbles Defense'?" Kurt asked. "I remember the experts talking about that way back in President Reagan's Administration."

Nodding his head in agreement, Blitz continued, "You hit the problem head on. When Bush I took control of the Defense Department, he sidelined the concept. When Clinton became president, nothing was done all during his eight years in office," adding, "My guess is they wanted to accommodate China. They did not want to offend China."

"If you think about it," Kurt intoned, "when the missile is first launched, you then know who the enemy is. Also, as the launch stage would be when the missile is at its slowest, it is easier to destroy, and it also would blow up over the enemy's own land. Any damage would affect him only."

"You got it," Blitz answered. "We have done extensive tests on the Brilliant Pebbles Defense, going back to the early 90's, before it was sidelined."

Kurt again shook his head in disgust, commenting, "That is traitorous, to say the least."

"We do not have the time or space," Blitz declared, "to survive any Pearl Harbor type missile nuclear attack. Back then we had the time to rebuild to defend America. Now we do not."

"Why aren't the so-called guardians of America, the press and the TV media, telling America about this terrible lack of preparedness?" Kurt responded. "As a matter of fact, why are not the American people charging Congress with pitchforks?"

Blitz shrugged his shoulders, commenting, "The American people are not the same, this generation, as they were in past generations."

Kurt concluded, as his lady friend returned from her kitchen, saying, "I hope that is not true."

Their hostess, who also was carrying three plates of apple pie slices, along with a decanter of fresh coffee, interposed, "I thought you might want to take a break from discussing such deep topics, as I was able to over hear."

Kurt hurriedly got up from the table to help his lady friend with her delicious burden.

Blitz smiled at the thought of such an unexpected treat, and told Kurt, as a final admonition, "I am not a Yankee fan, but I do enjoy the unusual truisms of Yogi Berra," adding, "He is quoted as saying, 'You can see a lot by looking.' That seems to me that covers it all."

CHAPTER III
HOBSON'S CHOICE

The following week, March 27, 2005, Kurt was back at his mountain, pulling his regular duties. Kurt's mind, however, kept pondering the disquieting cyber-defense situation that he and Blitz had hashed over.

The failure of our political leaders to put foremost the defense of the American people bothered him. During one of the rest – coffee break periods, Kurt related his fears to his supervising Major.

The Major, sipping his coffee, nodded his head in agreement, commenting, "We know that China is still developing its anti-ballistic missile systems, even though its leaders swore that it was not being pursued by them way back in the 1960's," adding, "We also know that China has developed, tested, and deployed a new, purloined, anti-satellite missile they call the SC-19. It operates for use in their mobile missile sites."

"If we know that," Kurt replied, shaking his head, "why don't we defend against them?"

"The Senate leaders, who are also mostly globalists, and the CEO's who run the outsourcing, globalist, American international corporations, don't want to offend China."

"Sounds like they are more interested in money, than in America," Kurt commented.

"The intelligence people I talk to," the Major responded, "think that what China says is only a clever propaganda campaign, designed to delay the implementation of our cyberspace defenses."

"It sounds like China has succeeded," Kurt intoned. "Beyond their wildest dreams, that is if they do have dreams."

The Major laughed, and then taking a big swallow of the cooled-off coffee, said, "There is a controlling, classified, National Security Presidential Directive that is dated June 20, 2003. It specifically directs that our intelligence officers provide continuous strategic, and tactical, warnings, along with their assessment of this information, to the president and to our appropriate military commanders."

The Major continued, "The Directive also warns that various enemies have shown the capability, and the willingness, to attack America. It clearly states that one of the prime targets, for such enemies using nuclear weapons, would be our nuclear defense installations, like our Cheyenne Mountain," adding, ""It also states that appropriate protection for such critical equipment must be to make them survivable, and to be capable of timely warnings of any impending action."

The major continued, "It also clearly directs, 'Facilities should be designed to survive, and to operate following any nuclear attack.'"

"That seems to be a step in the right direction," Kurt acknowledged. "The president, to enforce it, should publicly condemn those who do not want to protect America."

"My sentiments exactly," the Major agreed. "It does, however, looks like they are going to keep updating Cheyenne Mountain."

"What do you mean?" asked Kurt.

"Recall, just a few days ago, Admiral Keating, who is our overall boss, was here with a bunch of the media," the Major explained. "They were here to show off Keating's new digs for his 'Northern Command', which sector command covers the entire United States. It is being integrated, alongside NORAD, into our mountain."

The Major continued, "His personal appearance, and his touting of the facts that both organizations would work side by side, using the best equipment in the world, would seem to cement us as the premium defense location in America, and, as such, should have priority in complying with the Directive," adding, "My understanding is, by the addition of Northern, it will also require more and extensive new excavation of Cheyenne, to accommodate Keating's new, proposed, command center."

"I hope so," Kurt commented, "but the Directive does not specifically address our miserable lack of a space-based, cyber-war defense."

"The powers that be," intoned the Major, as he and Kurt stood, intending to return back to their computers, "have publically announced that the US Air Force will, shortly, establish what they call a separate cyber command, equal to the other commands, and on a par with Northern Command."

As both men walked back to their desks, Kurt pointed out, "It seems to me that just building more of our conventional weapons, such as precision guided bombs or missiles, is giving the American people a false sense of security. They cannot deter nuclear attacks, and their protection is puny next to a nuclear detonation. You and I both know, such blasts could kill several million people in this world, all in a very short time."

The Major nodded in agreement, commenting, "And we both also know that some well known foreign leaders would very well use their nuclear weapons against America, if they only had to respond to a retaliatory conventional response."

As Kurt approached his computer banks, he could see that some Air Force major was brazenly seated with his back to him, in his easy chair. He had both of his feet cocked up on Kurt's desk.

"What the," Kurt said, as he began a probable curse. This abruptly turned into a broad smile, as the chair suddenly spun around, and revealed the trespasser as his new friend, Blitz Jackson.

"Welcome to the Mountain, Blitz," Kurt blurted out. "What brings you here?"

"Official business," Blitz announced. "But I had to stop by and tell you, I mentioned, and only in the most general terms, some of your stealth ideas to a couple of officers I know, whose main jobs are new designs, and also procurement. I can verify, without a doubt, that they are strongly interested, if it is possible that your designs can be transformed into reality."

Kurt's face broke into a big grin, as he heard this report. He quickly grabbed an adjacent chair and pulled up next to Blitz, saying, "That is good to know. I'm not ready yet to disclose, to anyone, my final stealth thoughts or designs, but as soon as I'm ready, I promise I will give them to the Air Force, but only through you."

"That's a deal," laughed Blitz, adding, "What else is going on around here?"

"Same ole, same ole," Kurt responded. "I remain concerned about America's lack of a credible nuclear defense," adding, "My supervising major and I were just hashing over this pitiful lack of preparedness, during our last coffee break. We both blamed it on short sighted politicians."

Blitz turned toward Kurt, and leaning back, intoned, "You are right about our defenses being in the hands of short sighted, if not traitorous, politicians," adding, "Let me tell you the sad tale of a politician from Ohio, who happens to also be the powerful Republican Chairman of the House Energy and Water Resources Appropriations Subcommittee. He also filled that position in the 108th Congress, back in 2004."

"I'm listening," Kurt exclaimed, leaning forward.

His name is Representative David Hobson," Blitz replied. "He has represented his Ohio District for some time.

"He loudly claimed, for the edification of his public," Blitz continued, "that our nuclear arsenal remains an important component of our overall national security program, and he also says he is for maintaining our current stockpile. The results, however, of his direct, personal, congressional actions, in 2004, and since, did not bear that out."

"What happened?" Kurt asked.

"To get the full story, we have to go back to the 2002 presidential Directive, Nuclear Program Review, which called for assuring the continuing effectiveness of our nuclear deterrent. To do that, it logically requires that our nuclear weapons stay safe and reliable, and the only way to be certain of that is to conduct underground tests."

"Would that take very long?" asked Kurt.

"The problem is, such testing has been so negligently delayed, for so long, that even if we started right now, it would take some three years to do so."

"No kidding," Kurt exclaimed, shaking his head.

"Not only that," Blitz continued, "but the US is now the only nuclear nation that is no longer able to manufacture, on its own, what is, for short, called PITS. These are those vital plutonium cores which sit at the very heart of each of our nuclear weapons. Our political leaders, over the years, have negligently allowed US manufacturers, who originally, were the only ones capable of doing it, to close down. Relevant employees then either retired, or dispersed."

"We lost our ability to manufacture these PITS," Kurt intoned, "because our politicians failed to support and retain the American technicians who could make them?" again shaking his head. "This must have happened knowing that it eliminated these PITS, the most critical part of each nuclear weapon," adding, "Not only do we have traitorous politicians, but also brainless ones. Don't they value the lives of their grandkids?"

"Hobson just says, 'Since it would take years to rebuild, and redesign such a facility anew,'" Blitz pointed out, "'a little more delay won't matter' and also, that it would be an 'unwise and unnecessary use of limited resources to try to shorten the time necessary to again manufacture PITS on our own.'"

Blitz continued, "He also said, if you can believe this, that it would, 'send the wrong signal to the rest of the world.'"

Kurt stared in disbelief at this disclosure, and then interpled, "Hobson is only one congressman. Can't the rest of them pass the necessary legislation to retrieve, and revive, our nuclear ability?"

"Hobson claims that a majority in Congress supports his position," Blitz intoned. "That is a blatant falsehood. It is true, however, that most of the Democrats, and many Republicans, who put business and China over America, do support Hobson's view. However, when the appropriations for the 2004 Nuclear Program was wending its way through the committees of Congress, the majority, sitting in the full House, and also in the Senate, when each chamber was given the opportunity to vote on parts of that 2004, 108th Congress Appropriation Bill, did vote for the PITS and also for the underground testing provisions. Initially, thus, those vital appropriations were approved."

"What happened to them?" Kurt asked.

"Evidently," Blitz answered, "the congressional rules require that

appropriation bills eminating from each Congress when they get to the
end of a session, be put into what they call an Omnibus Appropriation
Bill," adding, "The congressional leadership of both parties then
appoints a joint overseeing committee. It goes over, and either approves
or rejects, each and every bill that has already been approved by one
chamber, but not both, or if they have to be reconciled. The majority
party, which in 2004 was the Republican Party, in both the House
and the Senate, was also allowed to appoint the majority of this joint
committee."

"It sounds complicated," Kurt whistled. "But the Republicans,
with a majority, should have prevailed."

"These joint committees," Blitz advised, "have been accurately
described as 'smoke filled rooms', and they really were at one time,
when smoking a cigar was considered manly," laughing, "The members
of the joint committee are typically the favorite political pets of each
party's leaders, and can be trusted to do their bidding, through thick
or thin."

"Does this story ever end," Kurt chuckled, "or does it go on
forever?"

Blitz smiled, proceeding with his comments, "We now get to the
Omnibus Appropriation Bill part. This is where the politicians really
show how they control things."

He continued, "The joint committee votes on each particular
appropriation presented, and either approves those they, and their
leadership want, or reject those his leader or he does not want,"
adding, "So when our particular appropriation bills, already approved
to rebuild the PITS, and underground testing, but requiring only a
reconciliation vote to clear up some minor, insignificant differences,
came up for a final vote in the committee, it was defeated."

"To quote an old cliché," Kurt, after a pause, commented, "It seems
it was Hobson's choice, and he chose wrong."

"Bingo. You hit it on the head again," Blitz intoned. "Hobson's
brainless choice was to reject and undermine this appropriation,
and thus render the maintaining of our current nuclear stockpile
problematic," adding, "Hobson's very wrong choice, in effect, took away
the voices and choices of the majority of the Congress, and also of the
president. Hobson and his anti-nuclear activists took away the choices

of the most important voice, the people's choice, and substituted their own individual agendas."

"Is there anything that can be done?" asked Kurt. "Does that committee really have that kind of power?"

"Once an Omnibus Appropriation Bill has been approved by the joint committee, the individual congressmen cannot re-argue it. They can only vote it up or down," Blitz explained, adding, "They always approve it, however, because it contains most of the approved goodies, the other congressmen want."

Kurt again shook his head in disbelief, saying, "It looks like the congressional controlling rules were put together for the pleasure of a bunch of dictators," adding, "It is obvious this was Hobson's wrong choice. It could not have been done, however, without the concurrence, if not the active agreement, of the Republican leadership. It is wrong. It is wrong. It is so wrong."

An eerie two minutes passes, as both Blitz and Kurt stared off into space.

Finally Blitz broke their mutual silence, asking, "Do you know the English 101 Shakespearian story called Macbeth?"

"Some," Kurt replied. "Why?"

"I remember a few lines I had to memorize back in high school," Blitz continued. "These lines came right after Macbeth murdered the king, and also his friend, Banquo, this was also after he, by many Shakespearian words, abandoned all his usual sense of right and wrong, saying, 'I am in blood. Stepp'd in so far, that, should I wade no more, - returning were as tedious as go o'er.'"

Nodding, "Nothing could describe it better," Kurt concluded.

CHAPTER IV
KEATING'S KAPERS

Kurt, through the spring, and the summer, of 2005, continued his computer apprenticeship, seeking the supervising Major's final approval as "Systems Review Expert".

This finally became a reality in August of 2005, after Kurt was given his final examinations, and adjudged an expert. He was now pronounced capable of operating, and reviewing, his expanding bank of defense computers, solo.

Relaxing somewhat, Kurt now envisioned a tamer work routine. He anticipated learning new procedures from, what he supposed, was the new expansion of Admiral Keating's Northern Command, into Cheyenne Mountain.

Now on his own, Kurt did not have his old supervisor to talk things over with. To compensate, however, he made friends with a bird colonel, an adjutant to the Admiral, who was permanently stationed at the Mountain to facilitate the anticipated Northern Command changeover.

At first, things seemed to progress on schedule. As September faded into October, the Colonel seemed more and more hesitant on committing to matters regarding the new Mountain Command.

Between drinks of coffee, the Colonel related, "Admiral Keating told us, only a few days ago, he is finding it difficult to be in two places at the same time," adding, "His NORAD Command needed him at the Mountain, for ongoing exercises, but his Northern Command underlings complained that he only comes to Cheyenne Mountain, not for change, but only for training."

"He is now located at the Peterson Air Force Base," Kurt responded, "which is only a twenty-five minute drive. That should not be a problem."

"The Admiral thinks it is," laughed the Colonel, "which makes it a problem."

"Then he should move his family, and everything else he thinks necessary, to the Mountain."

"Keating told us that only a few weeks ago, somehow, he lost communications, temporarily, with NORAD, during an exercise. He loudly complained that he was unable to be in two places at one time," answered the Colonel, laughing.

As the winter months cooled the atmosphere in and around the Mountain Complex, and also in nearby Colorado Springs, the adjutant's excuses for failing to start to changeover got more and more lame, as he then exclaimed, "The Admiral now has great doubts as to whether moving Northern Command to the Mountain would be wise. He told us at a briefing a few days ago, that a Cheyenne Mountain type of facility is no longer needed because the present threats to America are now different than during the Cold War."

Kurt responded, "You know that is not true. Our mission remains the same. Discover an attack. Find the Source. Destroy it. Plus keep the facility immune from destruction from nuclear attack," adding, "When NORAD was first set up, back in the 1950's, it was then first located in an Air Force base business building located in Colorado Springs. Officials moved it to the Mountain because, normally sane people quickly determined that such a NORAD Complex could be easily destroyed with only, 'one man firing a bazooka.'"

Kurt continued, "Everything still remains the same."

The Colonel did not reply, sipping his coffee.

By the spring of 2006, it was becoming very apparent to Kurt, and to others in the NORAD Command Center, that the so-called move to Cheyenne Mountain was now put on hold for some reason, still not explained.

The NORAD Commander, Brigadier General Rosann Bailey, who was soon slated to retire, informed her staff that she thought, not only was Northern Command not going to move to Cheyenne Mountain, but that matters were obviously in the works, to try to move NORAD, itself, out of the Mountain. A new location, at Peterson Air Force Base, was likely.

General Bailey further, with clarity, commented, "You can't make a glass building as resistant to attack as you can a facility in a mountain," adding, "I have a number of concerns about such a move."

Kurt's colonel friend was also suddenly detached, without explanation, from his transition job at the Mountain, and transferred back to Peterson Air Force Base.

In May and June of 2006, Kurt was given general permission by General Bailey's office to look over all documents, circulated by Admiral Keating's office, to all his Northern Command officer corp, and to other officers sitting on other command staffs. The relevant documents were entitled, "Point Paper on Cost Savings". The extensive Point Paper's main thrust was to promote Keating's idea to actually place NORAD, at Cheyenne Mountain, on "warm minimal" or "warm robust" status. "*Whatever that means*'" thought Kurt.

As Kurt continued to read these damning documents, he thought to himself, "These are Keating's points to set things to move the entire NORAD Complex from its safe bastion at Cheyenne Mountain, to an unsafe, unwise, place at Peterson.

"There does not seem to be, as I read the documents, any option to keep NORAD at the Mountain," Kurt continued thinking, now reading aloud, "The documents' main objective is, according to Keating, to explore alternative approaches to 'meeting the mission at a lower cost,' but admitting, there 'could be adverse factors that might be negatively affected,' however, the Commander would be 'accepting risk' to gain efficiencies.' How like him," repeating, "The Commander would be accepting risk," Kurt continued his thoughts, "What about the risk to the American public?"

But think great thoughts as he might, and ask unanswerable questions as he could, and complain mightily as he tried, Kurt was only a Captain, and in the scheme of things, not too big a roadblock for an Admiral. Thus, on May 28, 2006, the Keating ordered transition was, technically, completed, as a delighted Keating's Northern Command, and a dejected General Bailey's NORAD, solemnly announced that their operations had been agreed to be combined, and located at Peterson Air Force Base, Building Number Two.

Kurt did register aloud his severe comments, in earshot of NORAD's Command Office, saying, "The North American Aerospace Defense Command, otherwise known as NORAD, does not even have its own building. It has been relegated to the basement of a very vulnerable office building. Keating does not give NORAD value."

General Bailey's staff at the Mountain, mostly agreed with Kurt, but, when the top commanding officer in their part of the world, and one who seems to have critical elements in the Pentagon, and in the Congress, on his side, what are you going to do about it?

"A bad decision. An unwise decision. A decision that will, in time, compromise our defense posture, and could conceivably cost the lives of millions of American," Kurt continued pointing out, to anyone who would listen.

The NORAD staff agreed with Kurt. It was obvious Admiral Keating was not going to let anything stand in his way, as the Admiral kept repeating the slogan, "Faster, quicker, and cheaper."

"He is putting his own convenience ahead of the nation's convenience," Kurt kept saying, keeping alive this unmentionable topic all through June, and into July, 2006.

Kurt also told those listening, "Those people contending that to move the NORAD operation from Cheyenne to Peterson, 'would have more benefits than costs,' and that the operational advantages of this move are, 'numerous and unmistakable,' are mounting blatant misconceptions."

During this same period, and before operations were actually transferred, Kurt heard the growing voices of many other Americans who objected to the move, including both government defense officials, and private Americans. They tried, in many ways, to slow the change process so, at least, some safeguards would be put in place at the new Peterson location. They valiantly argued, their numbers too few, that it was arrogant of Keating, and friends, to push for such a quick changeover, being so willing to put the nation at risk by backing the Admiral's plan to place Cheyenne Mountain on so-called "warm standby", while, at the same time, scattering several of NORAD's critical elements, and sections to several other Air Force bases, or as Kurt commented, "Scattered to the winds."

Kurt, seeing the handwriting on the wall, started to explore ways and means, for him to try to return to the private sector. His main reason, other than pure patriotism, for coming to the Mountain, was to be part of the unique North American Aerospace Defense Command. That reason was now in the process of being so compromised, as to cease being a good reason.

The NORAD staff, however, told Kurt to hold off. They pointed out that their continuing, vociferous, complaints were finally having a big effect, and were starting to bring in new adherents to their cause. The result, the Admiral not-withstanding, Northern Command did reluctantly, but publically, announce, "We are not closing Cheyenne Mountain. It will serve as an alternate command center with critical watch and warning systems remaining in the Mountain." The announcement added, "More than sixty people will continue to work in the facility."

The NORAD staff assured Kurt that he would be one of the remaining Cheyenne Mountain sixty, along with his, still relevant, bank of computers, alarms, and strobes.

The staff also told Kurt that in other Northern Command statements, they maintain that they are, "simply remoting, or piping in capabilities that now exist in Cheyenne Mountain, to provide a fully integrated command center for all NORAD, and US Northcom missions, at Peterson."

Kurt smiled at the obvious Keating attempt to mollify critics, but Kurt assured the staffer, "I will wait a bit. We will see what we will see," adding, "I owe it to you guys to see this through."

July 1, 2006, came and Kurt remained at his usual station. Eighty percent of his former Systems Review Expert colleagues had been, or were in the process of, moving to Peterson.

His former colleagues also told Kurt, when they would return to the Mountain for something, that, "The Keating way of piping in capabilities, and other information, from Cheyenne Mountain data, was not secure, and that such critical data could easily be deliberately, or accidentally, severed."

The experts also told Kurt that, "Critical military inspectors had cautioned them while they were at their Peterson Complex, that the inspectors had no real, factual analysis of the effects of the ongoing transition on NORAD's Integrated Tactical Warning Attack assessment," adding, "Which, in fact, is our number one mission."

"You mean 'IT-WA'," Kurt corrected, using the abbreviation used by the Review Experts," shaking his head in disbelief. "That is what our job is. It is what we do. It is why Cheyenne Mountain was created, to protect America from sneak nuclear attacks by any enemy, or any so-called friend. It is a unique connection in the use of a combination of satellite, radar, sensors, alarms, strobes, and other intelligence, to monitor enemy missile activity from around the world," adding, "If the inspectors can't assess that capability, it, in effect, nullifies our efforts, and America may find itself in a bigger peril than they realize."

Kurt told one of his visiting colleagues, "As you well know, cyberspace is a big, big challenge to America, mostly because we don't utilize the technical information we already know."

"Or give it to the Chinese," laughed his colleague.

"One of our biggest problems remains, to determine the origin of a particular cyber-attack," Kurt continued. "They are often launched using bot-nets of compromised computers, which actually could be owned by innocent users, located anywhere on earth," adding, "So, should it happen, who is responsible? Who is behind the attacking computer?"

His fellow expert replied, "We do know how, but we don't want to be displeasing to Mr. Hu, after all, we could lose business," smirking.

"Before all that,":Kurt, shaking his head in agreement, commented, "America is now the only global power on earth, seriously debating as to whether it should retain its nuclear deterrent. Some of our liberal leaders think we can just trust the lives of our people, and our sovereignty, to such tolerant nations as China or Russia, depending, for protection, on arms control agreements, and precision guided conventional weapons," adding, "A nuclear detonation within minutes, can kill thousands, even millions," adding, "They seem oblivious to those Barbarians in the world who would not hesitate to use them."

The colleague, shaking his head in obvious disgust, intoned, "Arms control agreements give unthinking liberals the opportunity to think great, noble thoughts, and to embrace an illusion to find an effortless security," adding, "A former Defense Department Deputy, a guy by the name of Schneider, described the effects of depending on so-called arms control. He said, 'It is analogous to the idea of fighting crime by reducing, and eventually eliminating, the police, while at the same time, signing agreements with the criminals."

Kurt, involuntarily, broke up the super serious discussion, emitting a long, sustained belly laugh, joined in by his colleague, who intoned, "It doesn't make any sense, does it?"

"Its not suppose to," interpled Kurt. "Just as long as it feels good, it must be good."

CHAPTER V
A JULY FOURTH TO REMEMBER

Kurt remained one of the few Systems Review Experts to still be retained, and deployed, at Cheyenne Mountain, as July, 2006, reared its hot summer head.

"We seem to have America's premier nuclear defense facility all to ourselves," Kurt complained to the one other Review Expert still on his shift.

"I told them, just like you told them, that I would not participate in such a brainless, strategic, mistake," the other Expert intoned, "That I would resign my commission first."

"There are only about sixty of us left," Kurt noted. "But we obviously made our points. The Mountain is still operating, and America is somewhat safer."

"A big, big point is that the ever-growing number of transition critics can now compare the Mountain with Peterson," the Review Expert declared.

It was at eight a.m., or 0800 hours, as the military like to say, Kurt reported to his desk, and to his bank of computers.

"What a heck of a way to spend the Fourth of July," he thought.

About 11:30 a.m., or 1130 hours, however, Kurt was suddenly stunned, open eyed, as the strobes, alarms, and the heat detecting mechanisms of his computers, indicated a missile had been launched, somewhere, and it might pose a danger to America.

Kurt quickly informed his Review Expert partner about it, and meticulously began the computer process of pinpointing the place where it had been launched, the type of missile, its telemetry, and where it was heading.

"Send computer notice to our NORAD Command Office, and also to Peterson," Kurt told his partner, who had not yet registered any of the alarms on his own computers," adding, "Tell them I'll monitor its progress, and give them a full report. I hope NORAD understands and gives the military full alert."

Kurt, with long tested know how, manipulated his computers to enable and direct them to bring in all information from the low flying defense satellites. It remained the satellite's canny and technical ability to designate, and to register time and space, and to pick up heat related disclosures, locating the source of each particular missile danger.

"I have it on my computers," the partner Expert exclaimed. "Wow, look at that," adding, "NORAD has just acknowledged our alarm."

"I see two more missiles being launched from the same area," Kurt announced. "It looks to me like they are being launched from North Korea. They are definitely headed east. Would you also tell NORAD that?"

It took just a few seconds for the crucial, lifesaving information to register on Kurt's computers. In that short amount of time, it told him they were North Korean, and that two or three of the already launched missiles, were of the long range, Taepoding-2 missile type, and have a range sufficient to reach the western part of the United States."

"NORAD wants to know if they should contact the President," his partner broke in, asking, "Does it look like they are destined for America? Are they a present threat?"

At that point of time, the questions were answered, as Kurt watched the two long range missiles suddenly take a nose dive and quickly fade. The other three, obviously shorter range missiles, had died a few minutes earlier, dropping harmlessly into the Sea of Japan.

"No," Kurt responded. "You can call off the alert. They just went swimming in the Pacific Ocean," adding, "I don't know if they died a natural death, or were executed," chuckling.

As all the computers reverted back to their normal status, Kurt, who had remained standing all during the ordeal, sat down in his extraordinarily comfortable chair, and fully relaxed. He leaned toward his partner, and said, excitedly, "Everything works. The heat sensors, the alarms, everything works. If this had been a nuclear loaded missile, we would have positively and fully identified it," talking gleefully, like a boy with a toy.

His partner, smiling, shook his head in agreement, commenting, "But, the question is, could we have shot it down if we had to?" his attention then diverted as his computer registered, "NORAD just sent a computer message saying they don't think Peterson was able to identify and track the missiles until minutes after we did," he announced, leaving the question unanswered.

General Bailey, who happened to be at the Mountain at the time of the incident, came personally to Kurt and his partner, and thanked them for first recognizing, and then positively identifying the North Korean missiles, saying, "I hope this incident taught the Northern Command a lessen. Their insistence on disbursing NORAD to Peterson, using cost savings as an excuse, does not hold water. It has not received sufficient Defense Department review, and it could undermine US national security.

"Keating, somehow, was able to convince the 'key people' in the Pentagon, the Senate, and the House that moving NORAD would save taxpayers millions of dollars."

"It is a myth that the liberals were anxious to grab onto," Kurt added, closing the conversation.

A few short weeks later, General Rosann Bailey, retired, much to Kurt's dismay. He wondered if the retirement was voluntary or merely to accommodate Keating.

A few days after her retirement, Kurt was able to talk at some length to one of her former Aides, still working in the old NORAD Command Office. He told Kurt, "Once the General was out of here, the NORAD Command, which was usually the best pick of the commands, was quickly downgraded to only a 'Directorate'," adding, "I can see Keating's fine hand orchestrating that move."

The Aide continued, "At a meeting of commanders, a few days before she retired, during which Admiral Timothy Keating was personally present, General Bailey raised several questions about moving NORAD's Missile Warning Center from Cheyenne Mountain to Peterson, and to another, its new proposed location at Schreiber Air Force Base, also in Colorado Springs. She told Keating, face to face, that she thought the move would harm national security," adding, "The General questioned how Keating was going to integrate NORAD's strategic, critical mission with the less urgent tasks of the Northern Command. She was also of the opinion that the training of NORAD personnel at Schreiber or Peterson, would not be equal to the extensive training given at Cheyenne Mountain."

"I can attest to that," Kurt intoned, smiling.

"Finally," the Aide disclosed, "she questioned the logic of thinking there would be the same level of security as there is at the Mountain, compared to the bare basement of an office building," adding, "Admiral Keating, then thanked her for her input, smiled, but allowed no debate, and, of course, did not change his mind."

The logic of such a careless move became very apparent only a few days later, during the last week of July, 2006. During this time period, Iran let loose with several missile tests, lasting over two days. It also included the testing of a missile, Kurt had identified earlier, which had a range capable of striking Israel.

The General's old Aide, again, when he realized the significance of the tests, made it a point to contact Kurt at his computer station, and tell him of a conversation he had with an old time friend, who was now located at Peterson, "He told me that some Israeli stalwarts complained to the Joint Chiefs that it took significantly longer for NORAD, at Peterson, to identify the Iranian missile threat, than it did at the Mountain. They were highly concerned."

Kurt laughed, saying, "I told Peterson of it, via my computer, of the multiple Iranian launchings. They showed up easily on my computer.

"Did they say how much longer?" Kurt asked.

"Significantly longer," the Aide confided.

"If Israel gets concerned," Kurt chuckled, "maybe we will get our NORAD back at the Mountain, quicker than we think."

"I told them that the transition has slowed the process considerably," the Aide interposed, "That the missions, once done by a single purposed, focused defense organization, have now been fractured."

"It is obvious to me, and should be to any logical observer, that the new NORAD location, housed in the basement of an ordinary building at Peterson, would be much more vulnerable to an attack by a determined enemy," Kurt offered. "A surprise attack, not only would, but should, be expected, due to the new NORAD's exposed, undefended location."

"Supposedly there was an evaluation done," intoned the Aide, "which assessed the damage that would be caused by a supposed Chinese launched nuclear missile. The missile was given ninety-nine percent assurance of total destruction at Peterson. Had it remained in its Cheyenne Mountain bailiwick, NORAD would have had an eighty-five percent converse chance that NORAD's vital computer functions would survive. The evaluation also concluded that the present NORAD location is vulnerable to many random acts of terrorism. As an example of what could happen at NORAD now, which would have been impossible at the highly protected Cheyenne Mountain former site, a student from Red China, here to study, or to work, was used. The student is highly committed to the communist government leaders in China. He has only to drive a rented automobile up to the, mostly unprotected, front gates of either Peterson or Schreiber. A hand carried bazooka laying in full view in the back seat. He has only to aim it at NORAD's building at Peterson, or at Schreiber, and NORAD would be eliminated, as a nuclear defense. It would be then a simple matter, for the surviving Chinese student, or a compatriot, sitting outside the base, to make a simple cell phone call to China, giving Hu the green light to launch his nuclear missiles, and it would be all over."

Kurt involuntarily swallowed at such a thought, and then, a few seconds later, pointed out, "Another easily created scenario; a Chinese national, who owns, or commandeers, an airplane, takes off from Colorado Springs' Municipal Airport, and causes it to veer into NORAD's building at Peterson, completely destroying the facility. It would have the same effect."

The Aide nodded, saying, "It is a scary thing. It does not, however, seem to scare our leading politicians, or our commanding officers," adding, "That is even more scary," he intoned as he left Kurt to go back to his office.

Events, and circumstances, proceeded as changed, up unto the fifteenth day of August, 2006, when Kurt witnessed some of his old Review buddies piling back to the Mountain.

"What's going on?" he asked the returning friend, as he unceremoniously plunked down at a desk nearby.

"We had a complete power failure at Peterson," he blurted out. "Everything's shut down," adding, "I don't know what caused it, or how long it will last, but the NORAD Command ordered most of us back to Cheyenne Mountain. I guess it was an attempt to try to maintain our normal missions."

"How are you going to do that?" Kurt interposed. "All of your computer detectors, and alarms, are at Peterson," adding, "You are welcome to look over my shoulder, if you want to. I'm still operating."

"A lot of the Peterson personnel were sent home," the friend responded, adding, "You are right. There is not much we can do here except get in your way, although I sure would like to come back here."

"How long do you expect to be here?" Kurt asked, moving over a little, to let his friend get closer.

I was told by some electrical engineers, who were called in earlier at Peterson, to try to maintain power, that Building Number Two was never designed to house the number of networks, servers, and user terminals currently in use since the transition. The way that Keating's Northern Command put together the NORAD computer set-up, they, without a doubt, added to the, already deficient, power structure.

"It was a disaster in waiting," the friend concluded, adding, "Admiral Keating always bragged that the changeover would save two hundred million dollars, but I think it has probably already cost an extra three hundred million."

"Not to mention the inconvenience, and the security concerns," Kurt intoned. "I worry also about a probable situation General Bailey was also concerned about. Suppose our NORAD computers disclose an unidentified plane approaching the US. NORAD, as we did before, at the Mountain, at Peterson, will scramble to identify it as our urgent and immediate mission, using all NORAD's resources. It turns out to be only a friendly airliner with a maintenance problem, which should have been handled separately by Northern Command. But because of the combining of NORAD and Northern, both have been jointly activated by the plane," adding, "What if this ploy is only a sly trap, designed to draw NORAD's attention, while an enemy is using the breakdown of our computers, to send their intercontinental missiles zooming toward us with nuclear payloads. Our NORAD computers are thus, so conveniently tied up."

"That would be a big problem," the Review friend acknowledged. "I guess the only real solution is to bring NORAD back to the Mountain."

"It is a very brainless, troubling, challenge. By trying to integrate NORAD and Northern, how do you not divert the effect of not being able to timely re-set the NORAD warning operation after something like that occurs?" asked Kurt.

"It is also very clear to me," the Review friend related, "Since the move to Peterson, NORAD no longer enjoys the level of protection it did at Cheyenne. Now, it would be so easy to lose our former computer reliability, either by theft, accidental destruction, misuse, or some other kind of easy to occur loss. The compromise of our critical nuclear discovery assets, is a given," adding, "I'm not sure what level of protection the Northern Command Commander is willing to waive, in order to combine NORAD and Northern, but it is prohibitively high."

"We are talking about doing great harm to the strategic capacity of the United States, and to the American people," Kurt replied. "We must be able to deliver a fast response to an enemy who is sending nuclear missiles to explode in America. It could kill millions of Americans in only a few short, critical minutes."

"I hope the powers that be insist that the Northern Commander, certify that he is fully aware of what may happen if this, so-called transition is not reversed," the friend lamented. "As someone truthfully said, 'The path is too smooth that also leads to hidden danger.'"

CHAPTER VI
FIGHTER PLANE E-XXII

Kurt, cornered all the defense officials he came across, and loudly complained to every officer that made his way into Cheyenne Mountain, pointing out the basic safety of America's premier nuclear defense, was being downtrodden and sacrificed, for no good reason. Kurt insisted to all that could hear that NORAD, not only should, but **must** be returned to the Mountain.

Kurt, gallantly, maintained his personal vigil, glued to his computers. He remained the same, during the balance of 2006, and into the spring of 2007. Often in support of his contention, he was able to discover alien missile tests, their location, and other crucial details, before those at the transformed, new, NORAD, at Peterson. It was to no avail. The deciding powers in the administration, the Congress, and in the Pentagon, maintained their solid "Love China Bloc" refusing to return NORAD to the Mountain.

Kurt, from time to time, would even complain about the NORAD situation to a passing member of the media, knowingly putting himself, and his Air Force career, in jeopardy by such disclosures. There never appeared, however, either on the air, or in print, any of his comments.

Kurt, and those few of his System Review Expert colleagues, allowed to stay, and to operate at their usual stations, were used as a counter answer to Admiral Keating's many critics, implying that the Nuclear Defense Complex at the Mountain was still intact, and formed, what they claimed, was a secondary defense.

Kurt knew better. The basic safety structure was now unwieldy, duplicitous, and subject to many errors and losses. Training was also inadequate, and, the once magnificent, computerized, defense system, was gradually falling apart.

Kurt, on his days off, still continued to work on the stealth, and other design work of the fighter plane, growing ever more auspicious on his home computer.

"Why don't I contact Blitz?" he thought, "to bring him up to date on my fighter. Plus, there might be an outside chance Blitz can suggest a way to bring NORAD back to Cheyenne."

Kurt, accordingly, sent a computer message to Blitz's private computer system, on the twenty-second day of April, 2007, relating, "When you can, contact me. Want to go over design, and NORAD."

On the same day, Kurt received the following reply, "Got your message. At Seattle now doing test work for Bowing. Will be free, two days, April 26th and 27th, 2007. Anxious to see you at the Mountain."

Blitz signed off, saying, "Happy Spring."

Precisely at 0800 hours, 26 April, 2007, Blitz walked into the computer complex room at Cheyenne Mountain.

Kurt was, as usual, watching his screens, and did not hear Blitz, as he had come alone, until the now, Bird Colonel, was directly behind him.

"Good morning," Kurt said, smiling. "Welcome to the Mountain," adding, as he, for the first time, noticed the Silver Birds, glistening on Blitz's shoulders, "or should I stand, salute, and call you sir?"

"Not yet," Blitz laughed. "Not until I become a general."

"My Review colleague," motioning to the Review Expert sitting at an adjacent bank of computers, Kurt interpled, "has generously agreed to take over my screens at noon today, and do so through tomorrow, so we are free to spend any time necessary at Colorado Springs, to go over my designs."

The colleague nodded, and smiled, and then said, "Look, why don't you guys go to the break room for a half hour. Have a cup of that stuff they call coffee."

Kurt laughed, "Thanks. We do need to get organized."

Blitz, a cup of beverage in his hand, took a long drink of the so-called Mountain Break Room coffee, and muttered, "I've had worse."

"When we get to my apartment, I'll brew up some good coffee," Kurt promised, and then asked, in a change of subjects, "What are you testing at Bowing?"

"It's a big secret," laughed Blitz. "Its an, everybody knows, secret fighter plane they now call E-XXII. This means it is still experimental, but I can tell you, even now, it's the finest fighter in this universe. It is much better than any probable fighter anybody else has, in service, or on the drawing board," adding, "That Red China has not stolen it yet, is a big plus."

"Give them time," Kurt smiled. "They are probably waiting 'til you get done testing it," adding, "Did the Bowing engineers use any of my stealth designs, or the tail assembly configurations?"

"They did," Blitz replied. "Almost totally. Thanks for giving them your permission," adding, "You could probably have gotten a patent on some of that stuff."

"Right now," Kurt intoned, facially overjoyed that his designs were Bowing used, "America needs it more than me," adding, "But I'm anxious to show you my new ideas."

"I would have been here two days ago, but I had to go to Washington, DC to testify, in secret, to a Senate panel. They were about to adopt, as part of the Fiscal 2007 Defense Department authorization bill, an ill thought out section, sponsored by the Aerospace Industries Association, which would have, in effect, outsourced to a Russian company called, VSMPQ, all of America's need for the production of titanium."

"That is crucial, new, strong, but lightweight, metal," Kurt replied.

"Right. It is very crucial for our modern military," Blitz replied. "Just about all the vital parts of all our new aircraft, armored vehicles, and many other systems depend on it," adding, "Somehow this aerospace section got slipped into the bill. If it had passed, the Pentagon could not build their new jet fighter, or the new bombers coming on line without getting permission, and titanium, from Russia."

"I thought that current law required things like titanium to be produced in America," Kurt offered.

"It does," Blitz responded. "That's why I had to go to DC. If that section had passed, it would have nullified the very law you are talking about."

"I still don't understand why the Aerospace Industries Association wanted it," Kurt asked.

"The excuse they used was that it put hardships on small contractors, along with creating other compliance problems they had, in following the law," Blitz replied.

"Patriotism must not have been a factor," Kurt intoned.

"The Kremlin, if it had passed, would also have had foreknowledge of the grade and quality of any titanium used in our weapons," Blitz commented.

He continued, "The titanium law has been highly successful, and is responsible for the creation of a new, homegrown industry. In fact, such special metals companies as RTI International Metals and TIMET, lead the world in titanium production," adding, "They have freely offered to accept much of the cost, over and above their actual expenses, just to maintain their unique, world class, specialty metals for use, not only on behalf of the public, but also to supply the needs of the military."

"How much does the military use now?" Kurt asked.

"About twenty-five percent, and rising," Blitz replied, adding, "There is no question, some problems of compliance have arisen among some of the smaller subcontractors, and they should be addressed. The companies, and my secret Senate panel, promised to see if those problems could be resolved."

"How did it all end?" Kurt asked. "I'm breathlessly awaiting," he joked.

"For now, the aerospace proposal has been shelved," Blitz answered, "but I'm not so sure the whole thing was so innocent. There are too many people in power who want to outsource everything."

Kurt nodded in agreement, as he and Blitz chug-a-lugged the balance of the boiler plate tasting coffee nestling ominously in their cups.

"Now that's better," Blitz agreed. It was now 1500 hours, Air Force time, and he was sipping some fresh brewed coffee at Kurt's apartment.

"I've got a few rolls, courtesy of my lady friend, if you want one," Kurt ventured, as he continued printing off his current ideas on his proposed new fighter. He had earlier downloaded the blue prints from his home computer.

"If we keep incorporating all your good ideas in E-XXII, it will soon be your airplane," laughed Blitz.

"That would suit me fine," Kurt intoned. "If you see a design, or concept, suitable, use it. Tell Bowing to use the ideas this time, free of charge," adding, "My next airplane, maybe, might be my time to create a retirement fortune," laughing.

As Blitz handled each of the downloaded designs, looking closely at the individual blueprints, and then setting aside those few he knew exhibited something significant, Kurt cautiously mentioned, "One of the main reasons I wanted to talk to you is, I am very, very concerned about America's first line of NORAD Nuclear Defenses. Not only because the Pentagon and the Senate refuse to develop a Brilliant Pebbles Satellite Defense, but also because, for some brainless reason, they will not move NORAD back to Cheyenne Mountain."

"I figured that might be part of the reason for my visit," Blitz interpled, "I agree totally with you. When I was in DC, I complained loudly about it," adding, "I knew that some of those subcommittee Senators have a fixation on Russia, instead of Red China, as our number one enemy, so I related to them how the Russians are now using their ancient, prop driven bombers, to fashion a new missile problem for us."

Kurt's attention became acute, as he heard of this new missile problem, asking, "What are you talking about?"

"Plastered on all the TV screens, and the networks, from time to time, are old pictures of the Russian TU-95 bombers. That is the one with several turbine driven propellers. It first came on line way back in the 1950's."

Kurt nodded, "Yeah, I remember."

"This old fashioned bomber has been cleverly re-created, and re-equipped, so that it now can be truthfully considered as a strategic threat to America," Blitz claimed.

"I still don't understand," Kurt blurted out. "How can an old World War era bomber be a threat?"

Blitz smiled, and said, "The answer, which also provides support for your argument that a Pebbles Satellite System should be set up, is crystal clear," adding, "Russia simply equipped these old bombers with some cruise missiles, which they call the KH-55. These are new, air launched, cruise missiles. They are also an exceptional cruise missile, capable of flying three times faster than anything we have, such as our Tomahawks. It has a maximum speed of nineteen hundred miles per hour, and a range of two thousand miles."

"I'm beginning to see the problem," Kurt acknowledged.

"All these big, lumbering, old 1950 bombers have to do," nodded Blitz, is to fly to a convenient spot outside of America's legal airspace, either off our Atlantic Coast or the Pacific Coast, and, while hovering there, if they become so motivated, initiate a surprise attack by firing their cruise missiles toward the continental US. The speed and range would get them, unmolested, to just about anywhere in America."

"And we could not stop them, not with our present defenses," Kurt intoned, nodding. "Now I see," adding, "That information should have lit a match under the Senators' rears, to, at least, start on a space based, cyber-war, defense."

"I hope so," Blitz replied, adding, "It is ironic that this old TU-95 MS Bear, with a cruising speed of less than five hundred miles per hour, usually, such easy pickings for our Air Force, has been transformed into this formidable, strategic threat, making them much more dangerous than their use was as only a bomber."

"They can fly two or three of the old TU-95's at a time, one thousand five hundred to two thousand miles off our coasts, in a reoccurring pattern. This is beyond the range of any of our fighter squadrons, and thus, it can be a constant threat, knowing we cannot get to them," Blitz continued.

"At that range and speed, the cruise missiles, if launched, could not be stopped, either by our defensive intercontinental missiles, or by our submarine missiles," Kurt admitted.

"Not only that," Blitz pointed out, "These new Russian cruise missiles are not just limited to a straight forward, predictable, ballistic flight path. Russia has programmed these KH-55's to cruise along the contours of the land over which they are flying. They can go up over mountains, and then swoop down to follow the bed of a river," adding, "Even if we had adequate defenses, they would be impossible to intercept."

Kurt nodded, commenting, "I had no idea Russia has such highly developed cruise missiles," adding, "From what you tell me, even our most sensitive radars, which are designed to enable them to go from a ground based intercept, and then hone in on an enemy missile, but only in mid flight."

"That is our big, big problem," Blitz admitted. "That is why I contend that maybe Russia might have done us a favor," adding, "Maybe those liberal Senators, who believe in mutual disarmament treaties, and of the concept that nuclear warfare is too awful to imagine, and therefore, they don't think about it, will change their minds, and put in motion, a space based, cyber-war defense."

"That would be the only way those Russian cruise missiles could be stopped," Kurt intoned.

Blitz concluded, saying, "A TU-95 can each carry as many as six KH-55 missiles, and 'intelligence' tells me that Russia has at least forty operating TU-95 Bears, so they are not going away."

"China, to me, is still the main threat to America," Kurt admitted. "Russia might be, but it would take a lot of continued antagonizing, goading, and scaring them.

"Do you really think the Congress will finally start to defend America, rather than continuing to outsource it to their money making global world?" Kurt asked, as he and Blitz got ready to go out for a dinner at Kurt's lady friend's.

"I don't know?" Blitz responded. "I do know that a continued failure to act would border on an intentional act of criminality."

"Don't bet on Congress doing the right thing, even in the face of all the evidence," Kurt intoned, adding, "A guy called Mark Twain once called it right, 'It probably could be shown by facts and figures that there is no distinctly Native American criminal class, except Congress.'"

"Congress won't really change until the voters change it," Blitz interpled. "That is the only sure solution. At least for a while," he chuckled.

CHAPTER VII
GERMAN TOWN

That evening's dinner, concocted by Kurt's lady friend, was, as usual, unusual and delicious. She had taken a delectable chunk of beef, simmered it in a myriad of sauces and herbs, creating an edible, veritable masterpiece, which along with its accompanying gravy, home baked rolls, potatoes, and creamed broccoli, took away not only the palates, but also the hearts and souls of her two Air Force dinner mates, who usually spent most of their eating time in non-descript mess halls, run, or over run, by hairy, obese, mess sergeants.

Neither Blitz, nor Karl attempted to say anything intelligible, until after all the serving bowls, and platters, had been picked clean, in second and third helpings.

"Well," the lady friend observed, "I take it as a compliment that I won't have any leftovers to burden my refrigerator," laughing.

"That was the best meal I have ever eaten," Blitz blared out.

"Better than my mother used to make," Kurt echoed the praise.

"I appreciate the compliments," she continued, "but you don't have to lace it with superlatives," adding, "Save room. I have a peach cobbler later for dessert."

She continued, this time directing a comment at Kurt, "You talked about your mother's cooking. Do you realize you have never told me about her, or your family?"

"Yeah," Blitz teased. "Maybe you descended from European highwaymen, or maybe aristocracy," chuckling.

Kurt looked at both of his table mates, laughed, and then admitted, "I really did not think either of you would be interested," adding, "I come not from highwaymen, nor aristocracy, but from good, old fashioned, German, farming stock."

Kurt continued, after taking a drink of coffee, "My great-grandfather immigrated to America in 1889. He was from a generations old farm family, and farm community in northern Germany. He came to America to avoid being drafted by the Kaiser. The Port of New Orleans was his entryway, and he then sailed up the Mississippi to Kansas. He tried to farm some land in Kansas, but after two years of drought, he gave up."

Kurt stopped, took another long sip of coffee, and after Blitz, irritated, commented, "Go on. Go on," Kurt continued, relating, "My great-grandfather then grabbed a boat out of Kansas City, and sailed up to an Iowa city called, Sioux City. He stayed there temporarily until he found there was no land to be had, so then he took a local railroad, which had tracks leading to extreme northern Iowa. The railroad authorities told him there was little land, but there was some available land twenty miles east, just below the Minnesota line. He was directed to follow a crude dirt road, and it would lead to a swamp. On the south side of the swamp, he would find some tillable land. He walked the entire twenty miles, plus the seven miles necessary to get to the south side of the swamp."

"So what happened then?" asked his lady friend, as Kurt stopped again for another extended sip of coffee, adding, "I think you are intentionally stopping on purpose," smiling.

"My great-grandfather fell in love," Kurt admitted, chuckling, "Not with a beautiful fairy princess, although he later found a good old fashioned, stocky, healthy daughter of previous German settlers, who he married, and began the Reitz Family Dynasty. He loved her very much too, but, he fell more in love with that beautiful, gorgeous, black dirt soil, which he found on the other side of the swamp. He had never before witnessed such soil."

Kurt continued, "The official records show, when great-grandfather went to the claims office to record his claim to a homestead, there were shown originally, the eighty acres of land resting above the water table, and thus, suitable for farming, while the balance of the one hundred sixty acres was in swamp.

"Luckily it was spring when he first arrived at his farmstead. He borrowed some crude tools, and was able to fashion a sort of cabin, with a sort of fireplace, and also to plant a few acres of borrowed wheat before the Iowa winter set in. The tools and wheat were the compliments of some of his German settler neighbors," adding, "My great-grandfather sired three sons, including my grandfather, born in 1907, all three of which he put to work improving the farm."

The lady friend, at that point, interrupted Kurt's tale, saying, "Hold up the family tale until I get your desserts, and some fresh coffee."

The short delay was welcomed, as both Kurt and Blitz, lit into the delicious peach cobblers set before them with an appreciative zeal. They again sidelined any further conversation until the important eating job was done.

Armed with a fresh cup of well brewed coffee, Kurt was then urged to continue.

"Great-grandfather died in 1925. Grandfather, at the time, was eighteen years old. His two brothers were older, and had already left the farm, and headed West right after the First World War. Grandfather decided he wanted to farm, so he made a deal to take title to the farm, agreeing to pay his brothers, and great-grandma, a reasonable sum.

"My grandfather was the one who then fell in love with the enticing black dirt. They all had, however, worked hard over the years, not only to build a good, solid, three story farm house, and several barns and silos, but the also dug several drainage ditches. By the time my grandfather bought the farm, there it was then, one hundred twenty acres of farm land, and only forty acres of swamp."

Kurt continued, "Also, by 1925, the county had fashioned a dirt road, which came down from the main east-west highway. This dirt road ran the seven miles south to near our farm, and then abruptly turned west, to avoid running into the remaining swamp. The road was built parallel to the north end of our farm, and it continued on for another five miles, connecting to another main, north-south, county road. This loop, which connected the farms of all the old German settlers in the area, was called the German Town Road, but it was mostly used by the young men and women in the area, for a 'Lovers' Lane'."

Both Blitz and the lady friend laughed at the disclosure, and Kurt, fearing he was becoming a bore, muttered, "Why don't we talk about something else?" He smiled, suggesting, "Like the beautiful spring evening."

"You can't get off the hook that easy," Blitz intoned. "Besides, our hostess does not often get such an opportunity to look into her good friend's family. She might want to invite them to a mutual respect function."

The lady friend refused to be embarrassed. However, to move things ahead, she stood, and poured new cups of coffee for her guests, then telling Kurt, "Go on. I want to hear more," putting her hand in a friendly fashion on Kurt's shoulder.

Appreciating the encouragement, and the new coffee, Kurt then continued his family's story, and its unique farm in northern Iowa.

"My grandfather married well. This time into a prosperous, nearby Swedish farm family. A daughter first, and then my father, born in 1942, were the result. The house, during this period was completely remodeled, and modernized. Also the family tore down and re-built some of the old barns to accommodate a cow-calf, Angus, cattle breeding operation. This pushed the remaining swamp into a ten acre pool of water, with twenty acres of resulting pasture on the reconstituted, drained, south end of the swamp and ten acres of good farmland on the northern end," adding, "Needless to say, my father was then one who also fell in love with its unique, black dirt."

Kurt at this point, shifted in his chair, took a new drink of coffee, and then inquired of his table mates, "Are you sure you want me to continue?"

"I'm fascinated," Blitz intoned, not quite convincingly.

The hostess, however, looking derogatorily at Blitz, said, "Yes. Yes. We want you to continue."

"My aunt, two years older than my father, in 1958, decided to open up a small grocery store on the, then improved, graveled, loop road, which ran along our north farm line," Kurt continued. "The family pushed into place, on the German Town Road, some usable parts from one of the old barns. This was the beginning of the grocery store building," adding, "It was then somewhat enclosed, and somewhat remodeled. My aunt was present for customers from 2:00 p.m. to 6:00 p.m., Tuesday through Saturday."

He continued, "In 1960, my father, noticing the grocery store did an increasingly bigger business, especially on Fridays and Saturdays, contracted with one of the oil companies and put in a gas station, which operated alongside of the grocery store. In 1962, he added a small tractor repair shop, and, as a result, spent more and more of his time, along with my aunt, in operating the resulting business complex."

"Business complex," Blitz muttered, laughing. "You mean a short stop in the road," adding, "It was not a Sam's Club."

Kurt, smiling, nodded, enjoying the banter, while the hostess, eager for more information, urged, "Go on. Go on."

"Both my father and my aunt married spouses from the neighborhood," Kurt then related, "My aunt had two sons and a daughter. I was an only child, born in 1972," adding, "By 1980, I and my cousins were put to work at the business complex, and by 1986, when I started high school, we practically ran it," adding, "Remember, this was in addition to also doing all the farm work."

Kurt then related, "My Dad and Mom, and I continued to live on the original farmstead, while my aunt and cousins, although half owner of the farm cattle operation, and of the business complex, lived on an adjacent farm owned by her husband's family," laughing as he looked at Blitz, "Too complicated for you?"

"Its got to be close to the end," Blitz muttered. "There is only you left," chuckling, adding, "Sounds like the Reitz Dynasty is becoming a rich dynasty."

"Not really," Kurt commented. "We were just a typical American family, whose hard work, and individual initiatives paid off," adding, "When all was said and done, the profits evenly split, taxes paid, and improvements paid, the remaining income provided a good living, in a pleasant place, but no riches."

"One more interesting thing," Kurt pointed out. "The farm owner on the north side of the German Town Road, across from our complex, started selling off a few lots to a few people who wanted to build homes on those lots. As a result, they also platted a few streets. As this was adjacent to our business complex, and the new houses increased our trade, we did not protest," adding, "These new additions were enough to put us on the official state maps as 'German Town', but the so-called town is only given an unincorporated designation. No expensive police departments or city councils."

Kurt then concluded, smiling, "That is the Reitz story. Unadulterated. The typical, all American family."

"Ever after we now know Kurt Reitz went on to attend Iowa State University where he became their topnotch, star, Aerospace Engineer. Then on to conquer the Bowing Corporation, and now the Air Force," Blitz interpled, chuckling.

"Tell me about your Dad and Mom," his lady friend implored, looking again, derogatorily, at this time both Blitz and Kurt for their disrespectful banter," Are they still in good health?"

Kurt, sobering, answered, "I'm sorry. Yes, fortunately, they are in good health and enjoying life in retirement."

"I have one more banter," Blitz interjected, chuckling, "How come you did not also fall in love with that beautiful, gorgeous, black dirt?"

Kurt laughing, "My oldest boy cousin succumbed to that," adding, "I fell deeply in love with the Heavens, and with the stars and the sky, and in the process of achieving those worthy goals."

Time had been reached, where the dessert, the coffee, and any further conversation were irretrievably lost to the hourglass, as Kurt, giving his lady friend a goodbye kiss, thanked her for taking care of a couple of old Air Force bums, while Blitz profusely apologized for any of his misstatements.

The following day, April 27, 2007, was wholly spent at Kurt's apartment. Both of them strenuously going over, in detail, the downloaded, significant, fighter plane blueprints Kurt had created, and which Blitz thought would be interesting, and usable, to the engineers designing the prototype, E-XXII fighter plane, Bowing was producing, and Blitz was testing.

Blitz took the relevant blueprints, along with a note from Kurt authorizing Blitz to have them, and to offer them to Bowing. He promised to keep Kurt advised of the progress of E-XXII, and of his flight tests.

Blitz also thanked Kurt for his hospitality, and solemnly vowed, "I will do everything in my limited power to get NORAD back to

Cheyenne Mountain. I have already informed many in Washington, telling them, 'You are imbeciles.' It got their attention, but did not do much good," adding, "Many of them are only interested in money, and keeping down defense costs."

Kurt nodded as he shook hands with Blitz in a good bye grasp, interposing, "Sometimes money costs too much."

CHAPTER VIII
"F-35 JOINT STRIKE FIGHTER"

Utilizing their personal computers, Kurt and Blitz kept in monthly contact with one another through the balance of 2007, and into February of 2008.

Blitz, during that time, was positioned at the Bowing plant in Seattle, Washington State, for at least half of that period, testing and designing the remarkable E-XXII (22) fighter plane.

Another twenty-five percent of his time was spent before Senate, House, and other government subcommittees, as a defense expert. He was mostly called by, build-your-defenses-now, Republicans, to testify on their behalf.

True to his word, whenever Blitz had an opening in testimony, or any other opportunity, he clearly called for the return of the North American Aerospace Defense Command, back to Cheyenne Mountain. Blitz also urged NORAD to be re-instated as its own separate command, rather than merely a directorate.

Blitz dutifully reported his "Cheyenne doings" on each of his monthly computer chats with Kurt's computer, pointing out, "There are just not enough Senators, Representatives, Pentagon agents, or bureaucrats, who are really interested in providing a solid nuclear defense for America," adding, saying in computer talk, "They don't want to offend China. They say they need them to buy bonds. They also think communist China is, in the end, going to be a good fellow.

What they want, most of all, is to engage China's one billion, non-existent, mirage consumers."

Kurt continued to lament the fact that America's politicians refused to defend America, although they did not hesitate to get us into Mid-East conflicts, but as he told himself, "*Blitz is doing more about our defenses than anyone else I know. I should be grateful for that.*"

In March, 2008, Blitz reported, ominously on his computer, "We have now run across an additional defense problem. The liberals, and the outsourcers, are trying to make the case that a fighter plane, like the E-XXII, while nice, is not needed in today's friendly skies, and is too expensive."

The computer message continued, "The civilians running the Pentagon are suggesting that the existing F-35, Joint Strike Fighter, could act as an affordable fifth generation fighter."

Kurt sent back his computer reply message, relating, "I can't believe the politicians would try to promote the F-35 as the equal to an E-XXII. It can barely act to complement the 22. It can never replace it. Does not anyone in the Pentagon know that the F-35 is only subsonic? It cannot hope to compete with today's world class fighter aircraft whose capabilities go beyond supersonic," adding, "The new fighter planes are supposedly designed to replace, not equal, the twenty-five year old F-15's and F-16's."

Blitz's computer responded, "I agree. The liberals have even suggested that the F-15's and the F-16's could be upgraded as a 'good enough defense'," adding, "They contend that the continued procurement of the E-XXII 'would be a waste of taxpayer dollars.' Both the F-15 and F-16, besides being old and outdated, are already highly vulnerable to Russian and Chinese advanced surface to air missiles."

Blitz's computer continued its caustic reply, "Another problem is that some liberal politicians are aiming US Defense spending toward former American defense corporations, such as Lockheed-Martin, and Northrup Grumman, which are now, considerably foreign owned. The current defense spending authorization includes a two hundred billion stipend for them, for sixteen new, outdated F-35's."

The computer then spat out a scenario which obviously weighed heavily on Blitz's mind, as it related a tale about "Air Force Chief-of-Staff, General T. Michael Mosley. The computer said he publicly informed the Pentagon that he wants defense to procure up to three hundred eighty-one of our E-XXII's. He criticized the present authorization of seventy-seven million for the F-35. Mosley also wants, as a strategy, to deploy, all over the world, a fighter like the 22, whose unmatched stealth features would keep all our enemies nervous. Another Air Force General, who is now retired, and can freely comment, said, 'Those in the Pentagon are, for some reason, trying to minimize the extraordinary capabilities of the 22. They want to cut the program. They also want to stop it at the current numbers.'"

Blitz's computer remained silent at the revelations for a few minutes, but suddenly revived with a vengeance, as it, in effect, shouted out, "Another Air Force General has admitted, 'Defense as a whole has been gutted - - - We are underfunding the military.'"

As if taking a needed breath, Blitz's computer again fell silent.

Then on a more calm tone, it began operating, as it related, "There is, however, some good news. Bowing engineers have adopted, almost totally, your design suggestions, and also your stealth modifications," adding, "They told me to thank you profusely. They also want you to know that they would love to publicly acknowledge you and the valuable contributions to E-XXII, but the plane's top secret status will not let them."

Kurt felt a welling surge of pride and pleasure, as this was disclosed. He responded with his own computer message, saying, "I understand. I want no public recognition. I only want my beloved America to be able to adequately defend itself," adding, "The 22 is the key to US Air superiority, now, and in the immediate future. It is not merely a nicety, as some liberals contend, it is a necessity."

Kurt continued this computer conversation, pointing out, "I just read an account of what was testified to at a recent hearing before the House Oversight and Government Reform National Security and Foreign Affairs subcommittee. It is chaired by Representative John F. Tierney, a Democrat from Massachusetts. He quoted two former Clinton Administration missile testing officials who brainlessly testified, under oath, about what they said were serious concerns as to the need for any additional missile testing. Chairman Tierney, also, was quoted as saying, 'Earlier panels had also provided testimony questioning the effectiveness, efficiency, and even the need for our country's current missile defense efforts,'" adding, "Can you beat that. This is the House Democrat Chairman, of the main subcommittee in charge of procuring a much needed nuclear missile defense authorization, throwing out to the public, such unthinking, 'I give up' words."

Blitz's computer responded immediately to Kurt's Tierney disclosure, spitting out the comment, "If you think that is bad, let me tell you about a certain defense intelligence government bureaucrat I ran across, who also claimed to be a former CIA analyst for twenty-five years," adding, "His name is Melvin A. Goodman. He contends that too much power resides in military hands. That the US must return to the strategic agendas of Presidents George H.W. Bush, and Bill Clinton, who he said favored significant reductions of nuclear weapons, the signing of the Comprehensive Test Ban Treaty, and enhanced effectiveness for the Non-proliferation Treaty.' He also says, 'The United States must end its development of nuclear weapons, and the deployment of a national missile defense, in order to return to the high moral ground in the search for disarmament,'" adding, "This is the kind of liberal gibberish that is very prevalent in the halls of power, in Washington, DC."

Kurt computed back, saying, "Since we both are trying to out do one another with fantastic liberal fairy tales, let me document a situation that is already in place. It is unbelievable. The implications of it are unbelievable. That it is allowed intentionally by US security people, whose main job it is to protect America, is the most unbelievable," adding, "The chairman of a group called the US China Economic Security Review Commission, whose name is Larry Wortzel, is compiling a report. This is a congressionally directed, and authorized, investigation and report. It deals with allegations that the Pentagon is relying on Chinese manufacturers and suppliers to provide parts and electronics for the Pentagon's equipment and also for its computers," adding, "Can you believe that? This is no bull. I swear it is the absolute truth."

Kurt's computer continued, "Wortzel's report details the obvious dangers posed by such a reliance. Surely the Pentagon and Washington must realize that Red Chinese government sponsored hackers have intruded on US defense computers for several years. Yet they authorized this stupid plan that has got to be the ideal set-up for Chinese intelligence. It is as though Chinese spies created it," adding, "Mr. Wortzel states, in his report, 'Components of Pentagon computers, and networks, are manufactured by, and in, Red China, making such equipment extremely vulnerable to probable tampering by Chinese security services. They can easily implant a malicious code in these parts that can be remotely activated on command, placing US systems in danger of destruction or manipulation. Evidence was also found which established that hundreds of counterfeit computer routers already were imported, and placed in US computers.

"Mr. Wortzel's report also complained that when he tried to interview the Pentagon logistics agencies in charge of buying these Chinese made parts," the computer related, "he was given the run around. I don't know who is running our country, Looney Tunes, or Chairman Hu, but they obviously don't have the best interests of America in mind."

"I can top that," chattered Blitz's computer. "Would you believe it that the US Commerce Department's Bureau of Industry and Security has a program which was agreed to with Red China, is called the Validated End-User? It has apparently been in place since October of 2007. End-User allows Red Chinese companies to obtain dual-use technologies without the usual formal security checks usually required for foreigners to get needed export licenses."

Blitz's computer continued, "An investigating group, called the Wisconsin Project on Nuclear Arms Control, run by a director named Gary Milhollin, has looked into the obvious implications of End-User. He issued a scathing report detailing facts showing that five designated Chinese companies are authorized to use the End-User program and, at least two have strong ties to the main Red Chinese military."

The computer's message emphatically continued, "The company called Shanghai Hua Hong N.F.C. Electronics, Co., Ltd. is actually a subsidiary of China Electronics Corp., which is a Chinese state run outfit that produces all the major military electronic equipment for the People's Liberation Army (PLA). Not only that, but China Electronics is also a crucial department or section of Red China's C 41, which is the command, control, communications, computers, and intelligence arm of the PLA."

The computer continued, "The second most suspected Red

Chinese company is called B.H.A. Aero-composite Parts Co., Ltd. This company is a joint venture company consisting of A.V.I.C., China Aviation Industry Corp, the Bowing Co., and Hexcel Corp. This Chinese company produces fighters, nuclear capable bombers, and ninety percent of the aviation weapons systems used by Red China's military."

Blitz's computer remained deathly quiet for two minutes, and then began again its message, saying, "I know what you are thinking. Yes, you read me right. One of the joint venture partners of A.V.I.C. is our own Bowing Company. I have been assured by Bowing engineers that any details of E-XXII are not part of the End-User program," adding, "I do have confidence in those engineers I have talked to, but I cannot vouch for other Bowing bigwigs."

The computer then clattered, "Milhollin's Wisconsin Project pointed out the obvious. Red China can, and will, surely misuse its access to the technology transfers that may be involved. Chinese military people are sitting in the generous front seat. To so easily get access to this technology without going through even the usual lax export license requirements, allows them virtually unlimited quantities of some American products in those categories that have long been restricted because of their military potential."

Blitz's computer then cautioned, "Hold up on submitting any new concepts or designs to Bowing, until I am fully assured of the security safety of them."

The computer then continued to relate, "Mario Mancuso, who is the Undersecretary for Industry and Security, of the US Commerce Department, defended this End-User program in a recent speech, saying that the two companies cited by Wisconsin, their activities, and histories, were examined in detail, by representatives of the Departments of Defense, State, Commerce, Energy, and the National Security Council, and they agreed that implementation of End-User was the right decision. He further said, 'There is no way to trade in China without some government affiliate,'" adding, "Can you imagine such stupidity in the people running our country? After a pause, the sane, clear voice of the GAO or Government Accountability Office, along with Mr. Milhollin, was computed, setting matters right. Each group detailed facts in a written report, saying 'The program has yet to produce the advantages anticipated by Commerce.' These reports also confirm that China is refusing to permit onsite inspections by US Security officials, and further that the cited 'companies have strong links to the Chinese military. In the past, they were identified in illicit technology acquisition, and arms proliferation.'"

The computer energetically continued, "Mancuso, brainlessly, tries to defend the program, and the Red Chinese as being misunderstood, contending they will eventually voluntarily agree to onsite inspections," adding, "But the GAO and Wisconsin insist the safeguards are inadequate. They point out that Red China has consistently blocked all interviews with, or of, any of the companies, without Red China's specific permission."

The computer ended its message, saying, "Any attempts to question those responsible in the American government, for the program, was met with silence, or allowed no contact."

Kurt, reading the last submission, reacted with almost unbridled horror, responded, "Thanks for warning me on my designs. I will hold them until you tell me to send them."

After a few minutes silence, Kurt ended his "War of Computers", punching out, "The obviously similar attitudes of Red China, and of the US personnel who made such grievous decisions as End-User, and now refuse to talk about it, reminds me of a similar directive issued several years ago, by the graft conscious Senator from Louisiana, Earl Long, who then told his staff, 'Don't write anything you can phone. Don't phone anything you can talk. Don't talk anything you can whisper. Don't whisper anything you can smile. Don't smile anything you can nod. Don't nod anything you can wink.'"

After a pregnant silence, Blitz's computer, needing the last word, chattered, "Chairman Hu, says, "Amen," ludicrously.

CHAPTER IX
BALLISTIC MISSILE DEFENSE

June 15, 2008, snuck up on Kurt without him knowing it, as he, mentally, lost days and weeks to his own Cheyenne Mountain Systems Review, labor of love.

He was abruptly brought back to a realization of his other, somewhat normal life, by an unexpected cell phone call from Blitz.

"Can you get a week's leave on short notice?" Blitz asked.

Taken aback, Kurt replied, "Depends. What for?"

"I have been subpoenaed by a Congressional Sub-committee to present expert testimony on the subject of cyberspace warfare," Blitz responded, adding, "I will be one of three, or four, Air Force officers giving expert testimony on behalf of the US-China Economic Security Commission, to the Listening Sub-committee. The main officer is Colonel Gary MacAlum, Chief-of-Staff for the US Strategic Command's Joint Task Force for Global Network Operations."

"I told you about that commission before. How does it concern me, and my obtaining a seven day leave?" Kurt responded.

"I surmise I am going to talk to them about cyberspace," Blitz, laughing, answered, "Plus I also want to talk about the American ballistic missile defense, or lack of. I need you close by to give me proper information and advice on the missile defense subject."

Kurt's eyes immediately lit up at this disclosure, as he realized it was a chance to contact, and to also influence, the controlling powers on this, his favorite topic.

"The Air Force owes me sixty days. I should be able to collect on a week," Kurt replied.

"I'll fly into Colorado Springs on June 21, 2008, at 0900. I'll be flying a twin engine Cessna that belongs to a friend of mine. If you can go, you will have to ready, willing, and able, and standing at the airport, ready to fly, if we are going to get to Washington, DC on time."

At exactly 0900 hours, on June 21, 2008, Kurt was standing, and waiting at the Colorado Springs airstrip.

Blitz skillfully landed the twin engine Cessna exactly at 0913 hours, and pulled up to the tarmac at 0917 hours. Blitz merely drew back on the throttle, allowing both engines to ebb back to a slow ticking of the propellers, as Kurt then scrambled aboard.

"How come you are late," Kurt scolded, laughing, "Just learning to fly?"

"The air currents over the Rockies made me late," Blitz chuckled. "I told them I was going to report them to God," adding, as he sobered, "We should be able to make the private airport outside of Richmond, Virginia on time. We do have until 0900 hours on June 23rd to get to the House Office Building, where the testimony will be presented. Colonel MacAlum's office, and our Republican Representative sponsor, assured me that they will have a car and driver waiting at Richmond, plus a room at the Watergate Hotel."

Blitz maneuvered the Cessna flawlessly down the single runway, and then headed east toward Kansas.

Once in the air, and after Blitz had notified, by radio, the necessary air respondents, who he was, and where he was going, he settled back in his seat, and then told Kurt, "We will never have a better chance for an uninterrupted few hours to go over, in detail, America's ballistic missile defense (BMD)."

Kurt looked around at the clear, sky blue world at fifteen thousand feet, and agreed, "It is truly an opportune time," as he then opened his briefcase, and removed his necessary supporting documents.

Kurt began, saying, "The first thing you should let the Congressmen know is that current authorizations for BMD are skimpy, compared to the danger to America involved. Let them know, we are also even more worried that the present Congress might try to reduce, or even eliminate, the authorized, planned expenditures, or development, of our current capabilities."

Blitz nodded, "Go on."

"I think you should also give the Congressmen some history, telling them the BMD technology has been around since President Reagan's Strategic Defense Initiative way back in 1988. The idea was to change attitudes from one of 'mutual assured destruction', to US hope of survival."

Blitz just smiled, shaking his head, muttering, "I suppose opposition could be chalked up to a misunderstanding about what is achievable with a BMD system, but there are those in the world, and even some who are residents of the US, who don't want America to be able to defend itself from nuclear annihilation."

Kurt nodded in agreement, and then offered, "You can point out that George Bush campaigned on the promise to deploy an antiballistic missile defense in his 2000 run for the presidency. He did, legally, withdraw America from the limitations of the Antiballistic Missile Treaty in June of 2002, which finally did allow the US to do some simple planning for BMD. While there was the usual criticism of the program from the usual critics, reaction to withdrawal, between the US and the former Soviet Union, was actually minimal," adding, "As you are aware, the US did finally deploy its first interceptor missile of the proposed ground-based missile defense system, in a silo in Fort Greely, Alaska in July of 2004, and have, thereafter, added more missiles there, and also at Vandenberg Air Force Base, in California."

"That is the problem," Blitz intoned. "It is a ground-based missile defense system."

Kurt continued, "The Alaska and California missile silos, now in place, can only protect the US from limited missile nuclear raids that might be launched by enemies who possess only a few missiles. The silos, of course, would not be effective against the thousands of potential nuclear missiles that Russia or China could initiate."

Blitz nodded, and then declared in a loud enough voice to be clearly heard over the noise of the two engines, "I know all of that. Let's get to the meat of BMD."

Kurt again nodded, and then agreeing said, "Right. We know, and anyone who really has an effective BMD policy in mind, knows that

America must have sufficient, current, defense authorizations, from this, and also from succeeding Congresses, to quickly develop, finalize, and deploy, a system that can truly intercept, and destroy, any enemy nuclear missiles coming toward America," adding, "In all ranges, and at all stages of their flight."

"So realistically," Blitz interposed, "we are talking about a space-based interceptor."

Kurt nodded, and then continued, "This is where the Congressmen will probably protest that a space-based interceptor is too politically hot to pursue, at this time."

Kurt continued, "You will have to appeal to their latent patriotism, if they still have any. Point out that America cannot be truly defended from any sustained enemy nuclear missile attack from a determined foe, possessing even only a few intercontinental missiles. The US can only be protected if we have fully in deployment, a working satellite system, which can then be engaged, to actively destroy any enemy missiles coming at us, several at a time, in various stages of flight. This, of course, is the Brilliant Pebbles concept. The concept has been known, and fully tested, since Reagan's presidency," adding, "You could then tell those reluctant Congressmen, if they expect their children and their grandchildren to continue to survive much longer, in this deadly, twenty-first century, they had better get humping, and authorize this space-based program now. It is literally only a few years away from the critical, to the super critical. It is very probable that the nation we know as America will no longer exist."

"That is a good way to get their attention," Blitz agreed. "and also true," adding, "I can also testify that the Bush Administration's decision to place ground-based interceptors in Poland is predicated on trying to expand its limited capabilities. Trying to get as close as is possible to an enemy missile source."

"You can also instruct them," Kurt intoned, "the Patriot Pac 3, and the Navy's AEGIS Systems are successfully tested and approved as full systems, but the silo, ground-based BMD, has not been similarly proven. It has not been declared operational," adding, "The whole complex ground-based system is still under the control of the contractor, rather than the military operators. Even after a full four years of experiments in the field, there have been no intercept test firings, for two years."

"I did not know that," Blitz admitted.

"America has been engaged in the BMD for over thirty years, and, although we are completely aware of all the necessary technology to build, and deploy, a proper and adequate BMD system, which is spaced-based. For various liberal, political reasons, we have not done so," adding, "It is truly a criminal act."

Blitz nodded in agreement, adding, "It is more than criminal, it is treasonous. It is the trading of money for American security. It is posturing of the worst kind. Should this nuclear disaster occur, and coming from an enemy, who we not only know is our enemy, but one we have voluntarily furnished to him, his missile knowledge and technology, and have even furnished the machinery they could use to destroy us, those Americans who do happen to survive will rightly line those liberal, money loving traitors up, and hang them from the nearest electric power poles."

"Lets hope our liberal politicians wake up before it gets as disastrous as all that," Kurt cautioned, as he looked out over the increasing cloud filled skyscape, asking, "Where are we now? Do I have time to go over another subject you might want to enlighten the Congress on?"

"We are coming onto northern Kentucky and coming up on northern West Virginia," Blitz replied, "We still have a good hour yet of discussion time. What else is relevant?"

"Our communist Chinese friends are also working extra hard to develop an advanced, unmanned, aerial vehicle, or symbolically, a UAV. This is part of their continuing strategy to combine readily available civilian technology, which America is conveniently providing them, and then converting this technology into weapons, and other military equipment."

"What do you mean?" asked Blitz.

"US intelligence people have discovered, surprisingly, certain Red Chinese official government policy documents, which clearly set up a special project to take advantage of the brainless, American, dual use policy. This time it involves military applications of the unmanned aerial vehicle."

Kurt continued, "The documents lay out the facts showing that the Chinese government's continuing goal is also to produce a high altitude, low speed, long endurance, unmanned, aerial vehicle. They hope to do it in the next two years, purely to aid and assist their communist military in such application as a nefarious, cyber-war aerial inspection, and also the detection of other US defense operations. It also can be used to aid and assist the Chinese in their electronic warfare, and in many other anti-US missions of opportunity," adding, "The communists have also, in these documents, designated its main weapons manufacturer, China Aerospace Science and Industry Corp.," which is a totally state run company, to be in charge of producing their aerial vehicle version for Chairman Hu."

Kurt continued, "China, as a helpful aid to its technology, has already been able to buy from our friends, the Israelis, the US produced and developed Harpy, which is an anti-radar drone. It homes in on a discovered radar installation, with an explosive charge."

"How does Chairman Hu get by with all this stuff?" Blitz muttered.

"They tell lies to willing eared American politicians. Promising they are only using UAV's for civilian purposes, for exploration, and scientific works," Kurt, laughing, explained. "When you have some Americans, whose main interest are in amassing a money fortune, and have no particular use for our historic American nation, or of American sovereignty, then they will readily reach out to believe those things," adding, "When these same traitorous Americans are somehow propelled into political and military power, and begin occupying US seats of power, this becomes doubly disastrous, particularly if they also have sufficient, high powered friends strategically located in the Congress to back them up."

"We should be in Richmond in about fifteen minutes. We will have to close down this highly enlightening, but also down heartening discussion," Blitz admitted. "I will, however, look forward to throwing these truths at our congressional blagards."

Kurt laughed, at Blitz's characterization, saying, "I will leave you to ponder this non-idealistic thought. It was first uttered by none other than Harry S. Truman, who un-embarrassingly said, 'Always be sincere, even if you don't mean it.'"

CHAPTER X
HACKING

After a perfect three-point landing at the outlying Richmond private airstrip, Blitz taxied the Cessna up to the Quonset single hangar, saying, "Looks like our sponsors were true to their word."

Kurt nodded as he saw a civilian Hum-vee parked in the graveled parking area, "I look forward to a good night's rest at the historic Watergate Hotel," smiling.

"Don't bet on it," Blitz admonished, as he eased off the throttle, and closed down the twin Cessna engines. "We are scheduled to have dinner and then to huddle with staff, from both the US Strategic Command's Joint Task Force, and also the staff of our sponsoring Congressman," adding, "Hopefully they, and we, will be in prime shape to then deliver telling testimony to the examining House, Congressional subcommittee on Monday, June 23rd, 2008."

"Didn't you tell me earlier," Kurt asked, "That a lengthy and disturbing report on our brainless China policy had already been submitted to this subcommittee, earlier, by the US-China Economic Security Commission?"

Blitz nodded, as he unbuckled his belts, and turned off the remaining Cessna instruments, "I don't really think many of the majority liberal congressmen, forming the subcommittee, have even read the report, or realize its significance."

"Or care," Kurt submitted, as he opened the cockpit door, and got out of the plane.

The ride to Washington, and the Watergate Hotel, was swift and sure, as the driver used, and knew all the shortcuts, plus, it was a weekend.

The hotel Watergate proved nice, but a disappointment to Kurt, who then was chided by Blitz, asking, "What did you expect, the ghost of Nixon as the registrar?" laughing.

Blitz was again, however, proven correct when he predicted the time would be fully consumed by the various staff.

The first thing both staff's warned of, and briefed Blitz on, now including Kurt, as his welcomed, newly accepted, and noted, associate, and one who, hopefully, could be counted on, later, to perhaps provide additional, pertinent, strategy, was, "The subcommittee will not be friendly. It will, in fact, be hostile. It is chaired by John Murtha, a Democrat from Pennsylvania," adding, "The free-spending committee, The House Defense Appropriations Subcommittee, while lavish in their largess to a privileged portion of the US defense industry, obviously limited their gratitude to those industries that have sweetened the liberal committee member's campaign coffers."

The congressman's staff then pointed out, "The defense appropriation monies, for Fiscal Year 2009, have already been approved by this Congress, and much of the defense spending for the Fiscal Year 2010 has already been earmarked for many irrelevant things the military does not want, or need, but they happened to be manufactured in a congressman's home district, or by a manufacturer whose lobbyists have made their mark and money known to the congressman," adding, "Murtha is completely dependent for his re-election on the Democrat National Committee, and also on Obama's help to get back in Congress, and will likely follow Obama's campaign promises to cut defense spending, but only in those areas Obama, in campaign speeches, describes as 'tens of billions of wasteful spending,' specifically described as, 'investments in unproven missile defense systems,' and further, Obama says 'I will, not weaponize space,' and, 'I will slow our development of future combat systems.'"

"Looks like Obama, and his liberal Democrats, wants to further strip America of any meaningful nuclear missile defense," Kurt blurted out, causing the briefing staffer to smile, acknowledging the comment, and then nodding, as Kurt added, "Love of China with its fifty cent labor, exorbitant outsourcing profits, and its one billion, supposed consumers, seems to negate providing any US nuclear defense, particularly developing a satellite, orbital defense."

"I like this guy," the staffer said, directing his comment toward Blitz. "Where did you find him? He thinks like me."

"We are longtime buddies," laughed Blitz. "We also think right, and alike. Like two peas in a pod."

"I am also aware that the US-China Economic and Security Review Commission is headed up by a very able fellow by the name of Larry Wortzel," Kurt informed the congressman's staffer," adding, "I'm fully aware, also, through Mr. Wortzel, that somehow the Bush Administration has permitted a phony communist Chinese corporation, which is really only the militant arm of the PLA, to manufacture, in China, computer components, which are now 'embedded' in computers presently being used by the Pentagon."

The staffer again nodded, a look of surprise on his face, as he continued his briefing, telling Blitz and Kurt, "Mr. Charles McMillon of MBC Services, earlier also told the Commission, in relating the history of China's meteoric rise to power, 'Beijing began by devaluing its currency in 1994. This was during the Clinton Administration. This, however, followed the admission of Red China into the World Trade Organization, by the first Bush presidency. The Chinese forty percent cut in their currency evaluation cut China's up front cost of exports to the US, plus China also levied a tariff or a tax on US imports into China. These unilateral actions, unprotested, gave the Chinese an enormous advantage in un-free, unfair trade. The results were, obviously, a trade deficit of thirty-one billion in 2001, four hundred one billion trade deficit in 2007, and over five hundred billion now in 2008," adding, "But more ominously, China used to make mostly textiles and toys. Now, with improvident US help, China makes computers, computer parts, airplane parts, and cellular phones."

"China, obviously, learns to make these products by creating joint ventures with profit seeking US outsourcing corporations," Kurt offered. "China then induces the US firms to bring over to China their manufacturing know how, and their parts making machinery. China learns, or, really, copies the same, and soon is capable of making the original parts on its own. This all at a fifty percent import currency discount. This will, of course, drive any US firm out of business," adding, "The last chapter in China's book will be that China will kick those outsourcing American corporations out of China."

The staffer intoned, "You got it exactly right. China now also has two trillion dollars of American money in reserve," adding, "As McMillon has also reported to the Commission, 'China is now in the position of being able to cherry pick the industrial crown jewels of America, and at fire sale prices.'"

The following day, in the hotel lounge, Blitz was briefed by a Task Force staffer, who, after Blitz introduced Kurt, included him in the briefing.

The staffer told them that the information the Task Force had uncovered was bleak. It established that China, already, could be so far advanced that the US might be unable to stop, and, in some cases, even detect, the Chinese communist's cyber-warfare capabilities. The staffer also was greatly concerned that most of the computers now in use in most US government offices, including offices in the Pentagon, plus their computer replacement parts, are now manufactured in Red China, and have been for some time.

Both Blitz and Kurt nodded in disgust, as the staffer then pointed out how easy it would be for the astute and able, Chinese security services to tamper with those imported computers, and also the parts, by implanting a malicious code system, along with a date or time, to be remotely put into motion on command.

"They not only can, but they will," Blitz warned, "and the US better be prepared for it."

"I agree," said the staffer, "and also the Task Force agrees."

"Is the probable testimony to be given by various members of the US Strategic Command's Joint Task Force to the Subcommittee tomorrow, substantially the same as was given to the US-China Economic Security Commission earlier, and is that testimony fully included in the Commission's report to the Congress?" asked Blitz.

"Yes, and yes," the staffer replied.

"The Task Force gave the following information to the Commission," the staffer continued.

"The Commission believes that China is devoting an overwhelming portion of its resources to all the various modern uses of computers, including cyberspace. China thinks that cyber-warfare is the modern way to conduct warfare, and that it is an integral part of today's world. The Task Force also thinks that China has the ability to carry out cyber operations any place in the world."

The staffer continued, "Chinese military schools now use cyber-warfare as their main topic, putting the old suicide charges, and big troop formations in second place. Their instructors now emphasize on how to inflict major damage on an enemy in order to cripple him, particularly in the opening phases of a war."

Kurt, at that point, interjected, "The Chinese military has always religiously studied US military thinking. One way they do this is by sending their future officers to our American Graduate Schools, those schools which specialize in US strategic matters," adding, "In fact, in 2000, there were more Red Chinese military personnel in those US schools than US military people."

The staffer nodded, and then continued, saying, "As an example of their economic strategic thought, Red China would surely target cyberspace targets in order to destroy, or set back, the US banking system, and the existing power grids. The US is now so dependent on computers to operate its extensive water, sewer, electricity, and all kinds of transport, all of which are highly vulnerable to the disruption, or destruction, of all, or part, of those systems, each of which could easily close down a big part of America."

He continued, "The US government, and also, equally, the US economy, both totally rely on, and are dependent on, the internet, and on computers to run both operations. It is therefore a most critical vulnerability. The Task Force thinks that Red China will take advantage of this extensive American use of cyberspace. They list four reasons why. First, the costs are low, compared to other operations. Second, it is difficult to determine the origin of cyber activity. Third, the US, as such, would be hindered in its response, and fourth, there is no developed legal framework to guide responses."

"What about the responses of self-defense?" Blitz offered, adding, "Red China has no regard when they hack for a legal framework. That is an outdated, liberal concept that puts America at a great risk."

"Does not the Task Force take into account the present Red Chinese hacking of all our computer networks?" Kurt asked.

The staffer smiled, saying, "I was just going to get into that. The Task Force told the Commission earlier, and it is included in its report to Congress, that in the period of 2006-07, alone, there was a thirty-one percent increase in Red China's state supported, hacker attacks on US defense networks. This amounts to forty-five thousand incidents," adding, "The Task Force thinks there are, at least, two hundred fifty to three hundred Red China directed hacker groups."

"It's much too easy to access US computer systems, and networks," Blitz muttered. "We must tell Congress this access must be fixed."

"Alan Paller, an executive with the SANS Institute, a security company for American private computer networks," the staffer continued, nodding in agreement, "thinks that several of American private defense corporations, such as Northrop-Grumman and Bowing, already have had their computer files hacked by the Chinese in 2007. He also has reported that he thinks, in 2005, China hackers stole all the technical details of the Mars Orbiter's propulsion system, and its solar panels."

"The latest China illegal hacking is to target the mostly unclassified US military information, normally found on the NIRRNet network," the staffer then revealed. "These computers deal with Department of Defense payments of all kinds, troops and cargo movements, medical records, aircraft locations, plus all military e-mails. China sees these networks as significant."

As Blitz began to respond to this part of the Task Force report, Kurt suggested, then thinking of the staffer's newly revealed Bowing hacker information, said, "We now must be super careful of our designs."

Blitz nodded in agreement, and then pointed out to the staffer, "It is also obvious that China's state sponsored hackers can easily feed dis-information into the NIRRNet network, solely for the purpose of disrupting and creating confusion."

"The report," interposed the staffer, "specifically includes the ease, and obvious ability of China to manipulate our vulnerable NIRRNet, which also gives them an overwhelming capability to delay, or disrupt many defense related functions without actually physically engaging them, which it could not physically do with only conventional forces or weapons," adding, "Our Task Force, and other defense experts further agree that China's newly stolen development of cyberspace tools give it too big of an opening over the US in modern cyber-warfare, and that Congress has to do something about it."

At this point, Kurt caught the staffer's eyes, and attention, offering his slant, saying, "My biggest concern is to develop an American space-based nuclear defense, which it knows how to do, but cannot get the necessary political muscle behind it."

The staffer nodded an assent, and replied, "That is also a big concern of the Task Force. Their report includes information on China's new threat to space. The PLA, run by Chairman Hu, and his Central Committee, as the report states, has made space a big part of China's military's command and control system, and Hu has given top priority to its intelligence gathering," adding, "In fact, in 2008, China has, we discovered, given top preference to the development of space weapons. The Task Force has reported information that China probably, already, has the tools, and the weapons, to establish an exclusive space corridor over China, closed to all other external satellite traffic."

The staffer then pointed out the ominous news that, "China, using stolen US technology, has developed modern, co-orbital, direct attack weapons, and, what are called, directed energy weapons, able to inflict damage on existing satellites. They also have the technology to develop an electronic weapon, which they can use to jam US existing space assets, including the entire US ground support network."

The staffer concluded, "Our report certifies that China's obvious cyber-developments, plus their growing arsenal of space assets, plus space weapons, increase the likelihood that any war between China and the US, which may develop in the future, will surely involve actions directed against each other's satellites, and other deployed cyber-weapons. This action will probably occur first, before any other type of conventional action," adding, "The report, in words of no uncertain terms, chides Congress to pay rapt attention to China related defense issues, and that the defense of America demands that a space-based satellite nuclear defense system must be developed now. Further, that changes in policy and strategy **MUST** be taken now, to ensure that US computers, including computer parts, are manufactured by American companies, or, at least, by a more reliable source, and the present Pentagon, infected computers replaced."

Kurt and Blitz thankfully stood up and stretched, from the long briefing, as the staffer shook their hands and told them, "The Task Force and all America are depending on experts like you to change liberal minds and to galvanize congressional support for this most necessary decision to authorize these crucial expenditures, now."

As the three were then exiting the hotel lounge, Kurt related to his companions, "This situation reminds me of a story told me by an old Iowa political friend of mine. It seems, back in the days of yore, there was a character by the name of Gideon J. Tucker. A newcomer, just arriving in Washington, DC, asked an attendant if he happened to be acquainted with Mr. Tucker. The attendant replied, 'All I know about Gideon J. Tucker is that it was he who said, "No man's life, liberty, or property are safe while the US Congress is in session."'"

All laughed at the characterization, as Blitz, paling, intoned, "Better also add, country."

CHAPTER XI
STONEBRIDGE ET. AL.

After a hurried breakfast, and running into "getting in the door" troubles at the subcommittee's hearing room, Blitz, along with his new sidekick, Kurt Reitz, finally were admitted. Blitz was directed to the hearing table, up front, with three other Task Force experts, and Kurt was led to a chair directly behind Blitz, where he could easily advise him, if need be.

As far as Kurt was concerned, however, it was the newly endowed recognition given him by the sponsoring Republican Congressmen, as their probable future witness to testify as an expert in any future space-based nuclear defense hearings. This new designation, highlighted Kurt's Monday, June 23, 2008, at the soap opera-like subcommittee get together. Sunday evening, however, and continuing on into early Monday morning, prior to the hearings, Blitz and Kurt maintained a continuing, raging discussion about the criminal un-defense of America, by the policies and views of the liberal non-government groups, and the liberal Democrats, and liberal Republicans now sitting in Congress, plus the liberal bureaucrats, who, over the years, had moved into positions of great power in the State Department, the US Trade Representative posts, and among the outsourcers that now ran the US Chamber of Commerce.

Kurt had begun the strident discussion with a slam at the Bush Administration for engaging the US Military in such a strategically dumb war in the Mid East and at the extremely high cost of over one hundred billion per year, or two hundred seventy-five million per day, to run the Iraq War, saying, "Think of how many strategic, Brilliant Pebble, defensive satellites America could have put in place with that kind of money."

Blitz was also busy criticizing the neo-cons running the Bush White House, along with the National Security Council, with their never-ending efforts to drive a further wedge between the US and Russia. This time over the current raging war in the disputed enclaves of South Ossetia and Abkhazia, saying, "The neo-cons, and the Israelis, who trained and armed Georgia's dictator, with the hope he could take over these Russian oriented areas, and further isolate the Russian people and government by pulling a surprise invasion of Ossetia, saying, 'When the Russians proved they were ready, and able, for this foolishness, and soundly beat all of them, the neo-cons, who originally were irate, because Putin has neutralized their buddies, the Russian-Israelis, who had been freely robbing Russia blind, stealing and assuming ownership of much of the loose, former USSR production facilities, were able to talk their stooge, Bush II, into blaming Russia for their self-created problems."

Kurt countered, pointing out, "This denunciation of Russia also came at a time when the Moslem crooks running Albania, in Eastern Europe, were busy consolidating their US backed brainless policy to further isolate, and to drive out long time natives, the Christian Serbs, from their original nation of heritage, Kosovo."

"Or to agitate and rile Russia further, trying to put the ground based, worthless, defense missiles in Poland," Blitz contributed.

"Bush, the neo-cons, and their supporters in the US government, plus the media," Kurt responded, "seems to always take the anti-Christian side. To throw their support behind Muslim Albanian criminals and drug runners, should be a no-no," adding, "But what really deeply concerns me, is this Russian folderol, is giving Red China a further opening in its undeclared war against the US. This phony Russian issue has allowed China to assume a forced leadership over the, close to Russia, countries included in the Shanghai Cooperation Association, Kazakhstan, Kyrgyzstan, Tajikistan, and Uzbekistan."

"Speaking of Christians," Blitz replied, "the Russians, of course, are Christian. Dmitry Medvedev is a strong orthodox Christian, and

I think Putin now professes Christianity. We Christians should be on the same side. We should be doing all we can to ward off the constant Islamic anti-Christian thrusts, along with the anti-Christian rhetoric of Israel."

"Bush II has practically turned the US over to Red China, which, after the Clinton debacle, in letting the Red Chinese, in effect, run America, in exchange for the Clinton's campaign loan made to directly by the Red Chinese Central Committee Chairman," Kurt muttered, adding, "Clinton's folks, still having considerable power, and beholden to China, even under Bush, indicate it makes no difference whether the citizens elect the Republican or the Democrat candidate. They still represent the, give it all to Red China, point of view, and that attitude will prevail."

"What do you mean?" asked Blitz.

"Aides to both campaigns have publically declared," Kurt intoned, "that the leadership posts, in their respective National Security Councils, and in other probable foreign policy advisors, as disclosed by both campaigns, will be filled by ranks of current key Asia advisors, now actively on their staffs," adding, "This means that the Democrat will probably choose Jeff Bader, and Richard Bush, both now with the liberal Brookings Institute. Both profess that Red China can do no wrong. Another probable Asia advisor, the Democrat will probably choose, is Wendy Sherman. She is a former Senior Aide to Madeleine Albright, and also a current Asia advisor to the Democrat candidate."

"What does she recommend?" asked Blitz.

"She has said, publically that the Democrat presidential candidate thinks that the US needs to be, 'actively engaged with China,'" Kurt related, "And further that we need a constructive relationship with Red China."

"We all know what 'engaged' and 'constructive' means," laughed Blitz. "It means no change from Bush II."

Kurt nodded, and then related, "Another probable appointee, is Asia advisor Greg Craig, who was a longtime Foreign Policy Aide to Senator Edward Kennedy," adding, "but what concerns me most is that the Democrat presidential candidate is relying on a former Michigan professor, name of Kenneth Lieberthal, who is presently, not only a consultant to the Democrat candidate, but who is also employed by the national consulting firm of Stonebridge International, LLC for his Asia advice."

"Is not Stonebridge the company owned by Samuel Berger?" Blitz asked. "The same thief and crook, Mr. Berger, who stole top secret merchandise from the vaults of the National Archives, and then hid them in his shorts and socks?"

"The same longtime crook," Kurt admitted. "He also happened to be the top National Security Advisor to the Bill Clinton presidency," adding, "I am also convinced that Berger knew about, organized, or instigated the Clinton-Red China campaign cash/loan payoff business, plus the stealing by China of the American 'Legacy Codes' from Los Alamos, and arranged the Clinton sale to Red China of six hundred super computers, all of which allowed China to suddenly become a super-military power overnight, and a big problem for American defense."

"What about the Republican?" Blitz asked.

"It will be the same as Bush II," Kurt replied, "if he should happen to win."

"I was told by Pentagon defense specialists," Blitz intoned, "that if the Democrat presidential candidate wins, there will probably be defense funding cuts, and also modifications in the area of US strategic missile defenses."

"The Democrat has orated publicly," Kurt responded. "He thinks some missile defenses are unworkable. However, those used to counter Iran and North Korea are somehow, workable," adding, "One of his main campaign advisors, John Holms, who was a former Arms Control and Disarmament Advisor, told the Arms Control Association, in a speech recently, that the Democrat would limit strategic missile defense to only the current deployments, now in Alaska, and California. He also told the Association that, 'It is very important to proceed on the basis of workable defenses.'", adding, "What does that mean?"

Kurt continued, "Holms also said that missile defense should focus on short range, and local defenses, declaring that the Democrat candidates announced priority, will be theatre or regional defense, until, as he says, "The longer range technology is proven," adding, "The candidate also has stated, publicly, 'A missile attack is less likely than a nuclear blast carried out from a suitcase, boxcar, or shipping container, smuggled into the country."

"If that is what he really thinks," Blitz countered, "America is in real trouble."

"John Holms also led the Bill Clinton Administration's efforts to expand and extend the old 1972, Antiballistic Missile Treaty," Kurt then responded. "Thank God, he was not able to," adding, "Nullifying that treaty was, at least, one good thing Bush II was able to accomplish."

"This Holms is a real dangerous, beauty," Blitz muttered. "I sure hope he stays out of power."

"He could well be revived, and resuscitated," Kurt intoned. "Holmes consistently opposed both long and short range missile defenses during Clinton sponsored, inter-agency discussions, and predictably, he always favored the use of existing arms agreements over the development of any proposed new military, missile defense hardware," adding, "John Holms is the liberals' ideal, dream man. One who has a well-known history of posturing the US into a position of creating no nuclear, missile defense."

"In fact," Blitz commented, "he represents the concept of no defense at all," adding, "But I'm also concerned about Samuel Berger's consulting firm, Stonebridge. Isn't that the top US-China outsourcing outfit, and the prime consulting company that sets up China First things, like the current, made in China, computers and parts, and the existing dual purpose phony programs, and policies, that deliver to Red China, American technical data, supposedly for peaceful civilian purposes, and then assume those communist anti-American cutthroats, will only use the data for peace. Not give it to their military?" chuckling.

Kurt laughed at the length of Blitz's question, nodding yes, several times through each statement, and then, finally, at the question's end, declaring, "That is right. You got it," adding, "Berger, with his propensity to think of China first, is the favorite American of Chairman Hu. Berger can do no wrong. The China door is always open to Berger," adding, "American outsourcing corporations, and China loving politicians, and Pentagoners, who anxiously want to do things in China, know that by using Stonebridge, they are very likely to be welcomed by the Chinese leaders with open arms, and brought into their inner circle."

"I would judge Samuel Berger is also salting away lots of dollars with such overpowering influence," Blitz intoned.

Those statements closed out their Sunday night, early morning Monday argument soliloquy as Kurt commented, "The liberals in the Congress can also expect to be backed up by the congressional Black Leadership Forum, which wants the current defense authorizations to be quashed, in order to pay Black citizen oriented government programs. Also the Democrat candidate can be expected to pick such Brookings Institute liberals as Phillip Gordon, and Ivo Daalder, two so-called defense experts, as part of his presidential staff," adding, as Kurt and Blitz exited the hotel, "Daalder wants to, unilaterally, reduce the US nuclear weapons stockpile, regardless of the China, or Russian, intentional buildups." Kurt offered those final disclosures as the two proceeded to walk from the Watergate to Capitol Hill.

Blitz and Kurt, at first stopped at the Subcommittee's Hearing Room door by the Sergeant-at-Arms guarding it, and unable to enter until Blitz got his new credentials from his sponsoring subcommittee Republican congressman, were now the focus of attention as Blitz, in his turn, began to testify.

Blitz, and the two other Task Force witnesses did well under questioning, expertly pointing out the extreme and urgent need for Congress to take a fresh look at Red China's war-like actions, and to perceive of all the ramifications of its cyberspace buildup, along with American's self-imposed, lack of the same.

Kurt listened, as each witness succinctly, yet obtrusively, berated their liberal congressional questioners, accusing the salons of a failure to enact rational policies, or to implement programs which would provide the US with even the very minimum of a cyberspace, satellite based, missile defense, plus all the needed additions to the existing nuclear defense system.

Kurt smiled as Blitz deftly needled the liberals for having authorized, and then failed, to stop the production of, along with the import of, and particularly the Pentagon use of vulnerable computers and their replacement parts, directly from known Red Chinese military backed, state corporations.

The numerous, blistering, accusations, however, seemed to have no damning effect on these liberal congressmen, nor did the media present, even seem to take note as to the vivid disclosures.

As the hearing went into its first short recess, Kurt huddled with Blitz, muttering, "These blanket-blank traitors don't seem to have a patriotic bone in their body. Our experts' pointed, anti-American charges seem to rub right off. They just have no real concept of a traditional, sovereign America, governed by the people as a Republic. They can only think of money, money, money," adding, "It also reminds me of an interview Vice President Cheney had with cable's George Stephanopoulos, a few months ago."

Kurt continued, "George asked Cheney, probably leading up to a softball question, as to the Vice President's opinion of the fact that two-thirds of the American people, polled, were strongly against our Mid East interventions, particularly in Iraq? Cheney's answer, reflects the current overbearing attitude, both those in the Bush Administration, and also in the liberal majority, now infecting Congress, as to what they think of the American people."

Kurt paused, and then commented, "Cheney's answer was to use the single word, 'So?' His question's answer says so much, so very, very much about how Cheney, and other politicians, view citizens, and who now occupy both party power positions. They just don't give a damn for the people."

"Except when they want their vote," Blitz concluded.

CHAPTER XII
NO HEARING HEARING

The Subcommittee Chairman, Democrat John Murtha, having given his staff sufficient time to go over some of the statements made, and to review the allegations thrown at the several liberal congressmen occupying seats on his Defense Appropriation Subcommittee, felt confidant in recalling the congressional group back into session.

It was a late 2:00 p.m., on the Washington, DC afternoon of June 23, 2008, when the Murtha gavel re-fell, reopening the hearing.

Blitz and Kurt had not been negligent during the recess time, and had gone over several defense items with the Task Force staff, and also the Republican congressman's staff. Blitz was ready to "blitz" the Subcommittee, as the liberal salons returned to their questioning.

"The US Air Force now has one hundred eighty-three, on line F-22's," the next liberal congressman declared, "at a per each F-22 cost of one hundred sixty million dollars. Don't you agree that all that defense money could be better used in some other capacity?"

Blitz replied, "Sir, there are only forty combat ready F-22's now available to the US Air Force, and they are all stationed at Fort Langley Air Force Base here in Virginia," adding, "Both the advisors in the White House, and General T. Michael Moseley have testified that the numbers of the F-22, not only should, but **must** be increased to three hundred eighty-one operational F-22's."

"I understand the position of the former Air Force Chief-of-

Staff," continued the liberal salon, "wanting to enhance his office, by increasing the number of these expensive, redundant, fighter planes, to a total of three hundred eighty-one, but that does not convince me they are necessary," adding, "General Moseley mistakenly also wanted to station these F-22's in Iraq and Afghanistan."

"The General wanted the Emirs running those countries to understand that the US is capable of complete control of the skies, in the world, and also in the Middle East, if they equipped with the F-22's," countered Blitz. "The General knows that the F-22 Raptor exceeds the Air Force's operational expectations for this type of plane. The F-22 is, in fact, the finest fighter plane in the world. It is far better than any potential enemy has out there, but also any the enemy might have on the drawing board."

"I understand General Moseley was fired a few weeks ago," the congressman contended, smiling.

"He was unfortunately put out to pasture by a Defense Secretary who moves too easily by political maneuvering, rather than acting in the best interests of America," Blitz blurted out.

"You don't seem to want to make general yourself, do you, Colonel," the salon interposed, "leveling such outlandish charges at the Secretary of Defense."

"My only interest is what is in the best interest of America," Blitz countered, adding, "To fire the Air Force Chief-of-Staff over an incident that was solely the unauthorized doing of an underling, was only used as an excuse. The result is the appointment of an air cargo pilot general, rather than a fighter pilot general, as the new Air Force Chief-of-Staff. You tell me, sir, if that is in the best interest of America."

The congressman, flustered, intoned, "My time is up."

Kurt, noting his frustration, could not suppress a wide grin, as the Chairman then announced a second well known liberal congressman as next in line to question the experts.

Blitz, having been laid open by his opinions, became a, sort of, whipping boy for the liberals, as the new questioning salon asked, "Our Subcommittee has already authorized sixty-six billion dollars in Fiscal Year 2009 for extra use by the military, and yet you ask for more?" adding, "Don't you think the American people want to put an end to this wasteful spending?" adding, "Secretary Gates has already asked for seventy billion dollars more."

"Yes sir," Blitz responded. "I agree the American people want to put an end to wasteful spending, but I disagree that US citizens want to do away with providing vital national defense," adding, "Actually, the additional seventy billion dollars Gates requested, is merely to replace military equipment lost, stolen, burned, blown up, or warn out, in the ill-advised Iraqi and Afghanistan wars. I think total wasteful spending for those two wars is now close to a trillion dollars."

Not easily embarrassed, the liberal congressman continued, "You testified that Congress should fund Defense enough money to buy another three hundred or so of, as you testified, 'must have' F-22's. Are you aware that the Japanese military has recently cancelled plans to buy the F-22, and instead, will probably buy what they considered adequate fighter planes, such as the F-35 Lightening II. Some of our previous experts have testified that this plane is also sufficient for US Defense," adding, "The upgrade F-35 is produced, not only by America, but also by Britain, and thus, it also helps out ally. The Japanese are, in addition, considering buying the European fighter, the Typhoon, made jointly by Britain and Italy."

"Yes sir," Blitz again replied. "The Japanese have said they are backing away from buying the F-22 Raptor, only because the Bush Administration is now coming to a close. They evidently feel that a Democrat will probably be the next American president in 2009, and the Democrat candidate has publicly said he will likely curb, or even halt, the production of the F-22. If the Japanese military chooses to buy the F-35, modified or not, they will be unsatisfied," adding, "I cannot believe this Congress would fail to adequately fund this most extraordinary air plane, and deprive our citizens of such an available, necessary, fighter. I also cannot believe that this Subcommittee would intentionally put our fighting men at such a disadvantage."

Blitz's biting replies were making a big mark, however, the questioning liberal congressman, either did not understand the truth of Blitz's statements, or he felt strong enough in his District to disregard these truths, as he then contended, "The Defense Department's Inspector General, in 2006, issued a report saying, its investigation had concluded that there was undue lobbying in Congress for production of the F-22. He also citied the Pentagon funded non-profit, Institute for Defense Analysis group, as pursuing an F-22 program, which raises a question of conflict of interest."

Blitz responded, saying, "Don't confuse a strong desire to provide America with a proper, necessary, available fighter plane with the specious contention of conflict of interest," adding, "It is my understanding that all those who might be so accused, have resigned from any position with the Institute for Defense Analysis. I don't think it should even be considered as a Subcommittee problem. They should, if they are not now so doing, look only at what is in the best interest of America."

Blitz added, as an after thought, "The Institute has also suggested, after two extensive reviews of the F-22, and having endorsed its continued procurement after each review, that this Subcommittee should authorize funds for the plane, based on a three year contract. This small adjustment would make sure that our present American manufacturers can remain in business."

Blitz continued, "It is also common knowledge that the Democrat candidate for president, made it a prime campaign issue, in his bid for liberal votes, to drastically reduce US Defense spending. One of his most vocal supporters, a Democrat congressman from Massachusetts, who is also a committee chairman, has publicly stated that he, in order to assist his Democrat presidential candidate, would urge this Congress, and also this Subcommittee, to immediately reduce the Defense Department's present military authorizations by twenty-five percent. This twenty-five percent that congressman insists would eliminate any additional nuclear weapons, plus 'unproven' missile defenses," adding, "If these reductions are realized, and particularly, if nuclear weapons, and missile defense concepts are eliminated, the effect would be devastating to US security. It would, in effect, hollow out our military in a way not seen since Carter occupied the White House."

Blitz continued, "Not only would it place our citizens in great peril, but it also would further throw to the winds all of our US scientific people, whose technical know-how is necessary to accomplish these necessary defenses. Even more drastic, it would bankrupt, and eventually eliminate the US industrial infrastructure necessary to produce them," adding, "To do so would be extremely reckless with the destiny of America," adding, "The world is full of enemies, who are constantly working hard to build up their own nuclear arsenals, and their ballistic prowess, for the very stated purpose of destroying, or defeating, America."

The liberal salon questioning Blitz was unmoved by Blitz's cutting, telling, expert testimony, nor did he seem to even recognize the consequences of his Subcommittee's lack of providing such nuclear, and missile defense, nor did he even seem to care. He vigorously, and with relish, lit into Blitz, claiming, "You carelessly admonished us on this committee for not doing anything about these alleged deficient computers produced by, and in, China. I want you to be advised that previously appropriated defense grants, given to the Defense Advanced Research Projects Agency have been used to conquer that computer problem," adding, "The Agency has contracted with Hewlett-Packard to develop a system which will act as a counterweight to any enemy cyberspace threats. In fact, Hewlett-Packard was paid three point six million dollars to develop a controlling computer network monitoring system, specifically designed to protect against any problems which might arise from foreign made computers, or their parts."

He continued, "The Agency says Hewlett-Packard contends that its system will identify data distribution movement, before they enter the network, and monitor the same, in order to identify which computer exchanges could potentially be a problem for the US. Were you aware, Colonel that this monitoring contract was taking place?"

"Yes sir," Blitz responded, "The problem is current American technology already allows us to monitor, and, to some extent, identify computer hackers. The Task Force report told you, if you had read it, by using only present knowledge, monitoring known Chinese, state supported, professional hackers, whose only job is to continually lock on to US Defense computer networks. They have been able to identify those cyberspace networks as ones that most interest Chairman Hu. The Task Force also proved its ability to positively identify forty-five thousand hacker individual, Chinese computer hits. This was in the 2006 to 2007 period alone. Our computer problem does not need any more expensive monitoring, Congressman. What we need is some backbone, and the gumption to cancel those one-way computer contracts with China. Then, to take all the existing Pentagon, and government computers. Gather them up. Put them in a big pile. Salvage out any good metal, and then throw the remainder one hundred miles out into the deep, briny, sea."

The congressman glared at his contrary expert, as Blitz continued, "Anything Hewlett-Packard comes up with will be redundant," adding, "I do wish the Air Force had that three point six million available to apply on the necessary F-22's it wants," adding, "As an example of your alleged Chinese friends, I point to a nationalized, native Chinese, who was recently convicted of providing Red China with cyberspace related, American military technology. He admitted that he had been specifically sent to the US by Chinese leaders, to embed himself in an American industry that uses such technology. It began back in 1978, sir, and he admitted giving those leaders, the communists, such vital information since 1983. He had even been granted a Top Secret security clearance. I'll leave it up to you, and your colleagues to determine how that could have happened under our so-called security system, but it did. China will do anything it can to destroy America."

Blitz concluded, "Sir, also, if you will check around, you will find Hewlett-Packard is, at least partially, if not wholly, owned by state controlled Chinese companies. A monitoring system created by that corporation would be very suspect, don't you agree?"

The salon continued glaring at Blitz, and then to save face, thumbed through his notes, which lasted for several seconds, before telling the Chairman, "My time is up."

It had grown late in the afternoon of that fateful Monday, June 23, 2008, when, finally, the Chairman, informed the sponsoring Republican salon, who had briefed Kurt and Blitz, saying, "Its your turn, Congressman."

The friendly Republican smiled at Blitz, as he commented, "They tried to put you through a wringer, Colonel. If I was a betting man, I would have bet the farm on your testimony, and," laughing, "I would have won. You beat them back handily."

He continued, as Blitz and Kurt both displayed the widest possible grins, saying, "I also want to say I'm glad you were a constant reminder of why we are all here," adding, "Did you notice that, at least half of the media has now departed. They moved out when it was obvious you ran the last questioning liberal around in circles. I doubt, however, that any of your realistic comments will end up in the evening headlines, in the mainstream media, but rest assured, the truth will be disseminated, and read by many highly patriotic Americans. Did you also notice that there remains in this hearing room, only two other Republican members of the Subcommittee, and other than the Chairman, only one Democrat. I will not comment on that fact. It speaks for itself."

The Republican salon continued, "I won't go into most of what you have testified to, as it is already, graphically a matter of record, but I do want to comment on the F-22, and put my voice alongside of those who say, we must have this fighter plane. To stop its production would be, almost a criminal act."

He continued, "Every defense analysis demonstrates the vital need for this sweetheart airplane to maintain the US Air Force mission requirements. As you know, the F-22 is slated to replace the eight hundred or so still existing, twenty-five year old F-15's and F-16's. While these have given us a good air defense over the years, they no longer are able to do so, in today's highly technical world. Critics claim that they can be modified to make due, but that is playing hari kari with America's future. The same is true of the claim that the F-35 can also provide us a defense. The F-35, as we all know, can barely exceed sonic speed. Current surface-to-air missiles, such as the S-400 and S-500, HQ-9, and SA-20, possessed by both China and Russia, would make mincemeat out of them. It is clear the F-22 is an utterly essential component in assuring our defense advantage in the future," adding, "We also have an obligation to assess the likelihood of a probable conflict, sooner or later. We must plan not only for current conflicts, but also those that may occur in the future. We must have nuclear defense. We must have missile defense, but we also need a conventional non-nuclear means to defeat an enemy. The potential loss, in today's world, is just too great to make due with normal expectancy conflicts. We must do more. No nation, including the US, has the wisdom or the ability to predict what the world will be like, one or two generations out, but we must be prepared."

The congressman then stopped his conversation, looked steadily at Blitz, Kurt, and all the remaining people in the hearing room, and then stated, in a loud, authoritative voice, "The F-22 is America's equalizer."

Kurt could not help himself with that statement. He had to stand up and begin clapping. He continued doing so, as Blitz, and the Task Force expert witnesses also joined him. Soon everyone in the room, except the chairman, stood and maintained the continuous applause for over several minutes, as the Subcommittee Chairman, uselessly, pounded his gavel, calling for order.

The applause finally diminished, which allowed the Republican congressman to speak directly to Blitz, and ask, "Is there anything more you want to add, or to say, Colonel?"

Blitz thought a few seconds, and then stood, taking his wallet from his breast pocket. He rummaged through it and finding the saved piece of philosophy he wanted in its leather compartment, said, "If I may, sir, I would like to read this short passage from the past. It was written by a relatively unknown philosopher at the beginning of the eighteenth century. Its wisdom is appropriate today. It begins by describing the stages of civilization:
'From bondage to spiritual faith,
From spiritual faith to great courage,
From courage to liberty,
From liberty to abundance,
From abundance to selfishness,
From selfishness to complacency,
From complacency to apathy,
From apathy to dependence,'
Blitz repeated this phrase slowly, and then read the final phrase,
'From dependency back into bondage.'"

As Blitz returned back to his witness table chair, not a sound, absolutely none, could be heard anywhere in the hearing room.

CHAPTER XIII
REFLECTIONS

"How was the vacation?" Kurt's Systems Review Expert partner asked, as Kurt made his way back to his computer bank post, in the depths of Cheyenne Mountain.

"Interesting, Fascinating, revealing," Kurt replied. "And yet, parts of it were so bad, I dare not repeat them," laughing.

"Sounds like a girl I once knew," his partner responded, grinning sheepishly.

"I wish I was referring to the fairer sex," Kurt explained. "Actually, I was talking about the exalted people, the political geniuses we are supposed to look up to, who populate the US Congress. My God, no wonder Congress' standing with the American public is down to single digits."

Kurt then spent the next half hour going over his misadventures in the nation's capitol, going into detail as to the unusual antics of this Congressional Appropriations Subcommittee, stacked with well known national politicians.

"It was a learning experience, but also a once-in-a-lifetime opportunity," Kurt intoned, adding, "One good, positive thing to come out of it is I am now considered an expert on nuclear missile defense, and also on Brilliant Pebbles type cyberspace satellite defense."

The partner was smiling as he said, "Are you sure you want to go through that crazy stuff?" adding, "It is much more cozy to be embedded in this crazy mountain nook.

"I do look forward to spending a week at home over the Fourth of July," the partner continued. "I appreciate your trading with me an Air Force approved time off, mine to start July 2, 2008 to July 9th. I have not seen my folks in St. Louis for two years."

"They won't know you with that full grown beard," Kurt laughed.

"All kidding aside," the partner insisted, "I do relish the time off. I was getting stir crazy looking at these computers constantly," adding, "I did, however, find some interesting things to read while you were gone, during break times. They were generously furnished by the remnants of our remaining command structure, still occupying the desks in the Mountain."

"What was so interesting?" asked Kurt.

"The Command must still be on the 'receive unreleased reports' list, including one report authorized by the State Department. It contains what the Department calls 'frank advice dealing with the not yet released to the public assessment of China's war-like motives and intentions'. It echoes the absurdities, you told me about, mouthed by the liberal congressmen on your subcommittee."

"I'm all ears," Kurt grinned.

"This featured a several page draft report document, being reviewed by this so-called Advisory Board consisting of seventeen members, whose chair is, wouldn't you know, Paul Wolfowitz, and whose members include LBJ's son-in-law, Charles Robb; Allison Fortier, Vice-president, Lockheed Martin; William van Cleave, from Missouri State; and others. They made their initial conclusions about this government-private sector report analysis, 'that China's military modernization, though significant, does not pose a major challenge to US security interests.' The report itself, however, was put together by Brandon Buttrick and Robert Joseph, a former Under-secretary of State. Though the report is still unpublished, it did make some interesting observations."

"Anything headed by Paul Wolfowitz is bound to be interesting, if not worse," Kurt offered.

"Remember," cautioned the partner, "Mr. Wolfowitz is merely analyzing Buttrick's report, , he did not create it," adding, "The draft report says, however, that China's main military and commercial goals are to provide a counter-balance to the US presence and the US military capabilities, in the Far East. China is obviously providing a challenge to the US everywhere. The report then continues to say that China seems intent on acquiring a military prowess, which can be employed in critical areas, and aimed directly at the weaknesses of the American military; such as its failure to protect its vulnerable computers and cyberspace systems from attack and exploitation. Such a capability, the report continues, would allow Red China to be able to defeat a conventionally stronger US military.

"The Buttrick Report goes on to recommend," the partner continued, "that the US, post haste, fill its obvious vulnerability gaps. These, it describes, as no US missile defenses; US dependence on cyberspace; the inability of the US military to use force against China, except through aircraft carrier type task forces; the US's fragile electronics, and the vulnerability of its internet," adding, "The report also calls for the US to acquire new offensive space, and cyber warfare weapons, and capabilities, along with missile defenses."

Kurt starred at the partner, exhibiting an uncontrollable amount of amazement in his demeanor, finally blurting out, "This is exactly what Blitz, and the other Task Force experts told the House Defense Authorization Subcommittee," adding, "and it is equally descriptive of the attitude of the majority of liberal congressmen, populating the very same Defense Appropriation Subcommittee, including maintaining an obvious indifference to the dire consequences which could easily happen to America by their 'don't care' way of defending the US."

"The report," the partner continued, "takes dead aim at the proven, ongoing, industrial and defense espionage, of Red China, allowing them to obtain an advantage in technology for purely military reasons," adding, "The report charges that US security people possess only a limited understanding of true Chinese intentions, alleging that it is evident that Chinese military leaders, as shown by the People's Liberation Army's Communist Party, Political Standing Committee, including the Central Military Commission seems to suffer a paranoia and misperceptions about US military intentions."

Suppressing a laugh, Kurt pointed out, "Chairman Hu knows exactly what he is doing, as would any sane American security person," adding, "While I was in the capitol last week, I was told by a lucid security person looking into how our friend, Red China misleads.

Our Chinese first American friends, who are evidently endowed with permanent tenure in our bureaucracy running our State Department, and our vulnerable nuclear laboratories, constantly misread our relationship."

Kurt continued, "Although there was, and is, no specific nuclear, radiological or terrorist threat to the August 2008, upcoming Chinese run Olympics, the State Department, back in June, or earlier, which, under the Atomic Energy Act, has jurisdiction of deploying, what is called, NEST, or Nuclear Detection Teams, dispatched a ten member team, ostensibly to assist Beijing, in publicly unasked for, specialized technical expertise. This ten member NEST team is composed of US nuclear weapons scientists, plus technicians, many hailing from our nuclear labs, such as Los Alamos. The team included many native born Chinese, now naturalized Americans, as part of this technology group, providing this unneeded, never to be used, technical expertise. A State Department fact sheet says the NEST team will deal with the technical aspects of any nuclear, or radiological, terrorist threats."

Laughing, Kurt muttered, "What a big joke. The CIA, in May of 2000, back during Bill Clinton's presidency, made a determination that Red China, by an in-house, almost open espionage, was able to obtain details of every deployed nuclear warhead in the US arsenal. It was the computer hard drives taken from, ironically, a NEST laptop computer, protected, supposedly, by top security at the Los Alamos lab that was the culprit. It revealed to China our so-called nuclear 'legacy codes'," adding, "As an interesting, if not fatal, corollary to this story, it was also determined that a Chinese mainland born, naturalized American, and now a scientist, working at Los Alamos, conveniently had complete access to that very same laptop, and that very same hard drive."

"What a coincidence, just like Alice in Wonderland," the partner chuckled, "up is down and black is white."

"It is sometimes difficult to decide if Chairman Hu is really that bright and efficient in stealing our secrets, and technology," Kurt muttered, "or are our politicians and bureaucrats just easy touches to freely offer them."

"Money can create that kind of results," the partner commented, "or the promise of money."

"It will not be any better if the Democrat is elected in the upcoming

November election," Kurt intoned. "It became apparent to me, while I was in the capitol, that liberal Democrat congressmen, and equally, such Democrat campaign advisors, as those from the Space Policy Institute, and the Center for Strategic and International Studies, that it is clear the Democrat will downplay cyberspace, including creating weapons in space. His campaign websites stress that he wants to keep space assets free of disruption, and does not think it is good policy to confront China, or to call attention to any hostile intent by China in operating in space. He opposes stationing weapons in space, and the development of anti-satellite weapons. He orates that the US must, instead, show leadership by engaging in discussions of how best to stop the slow slide toward a new battlefield," adding, "and finally, he thinks the US should try to discover new technologies and capabilities that will allow US space assets to avoid attacks," Kurt stopped, looked at his partner, and laughing, continued, "Then the Democrat, implausibly states, 'Recover from them quickly.'"

"He must be willing to give the Chinese first shot," grimaced the partner, shaking his head. "He must not understand, in such a war, you only get one chance, and it better be first."

"Exactly," Kurt echoed. "Just to show you how far off he and his advisors are, they continue to mouth that the US should downplay the significance of China's 2007 ASAT test, which definitively proved China can shoot down and obliterate ongoing satellites in space with impunity. China is clearly in possession of such necessary technology," adding, "The liberal Democrats think by merely talking to China, they will not want to pursue further developments.

"To make matters worse," Kurt complained, "I also discovered that the US National Chamber of Commerce is also lobbying against stationing weapons in space. They complain that their lucrative satellite equipment, and the gear, and paraphernalia that goes with it, which they want to continue to sell to China, is put at risk because of a sensible US law, which may restrict American businesses from making those types of sales, its called 'Traffic in Arms Regulations' or ITAR."

Kurt continued, "Under ITAR, an export license is required if what they sell should become part of creating a satellite weapon in space, either Chinese or American. The National Chamber has a thirty-three member Space Enterprise Council, and they have registered continued ongoing complaints, saying that the licensing process under ITAR is lengthy, unpredictable, and inefficient. They also argue that these license restraints are unfair, because foreign companies, also engaged in satellite, and satellite parts sales don't have to deal with export licenses."

"What about if China creates its own satellite weapons, and then uses them to destroy the computer, telephone, radio, and any other means of communication, of these same American companies," the partner interposed. "It seems like a reasonable thing to require licensing."

Kurt nodded in agreement, saying, "The US satellite companies are mad because ITAR blocks them from accessing the low cost satellite launch vehicles which China now offers at cut rates. Smart guys these Chinese."

"Dumb guys," the partner echoed, "those money hungry Americans."

"Another dumb American proposal," Kurt commented, "is rather than develop a Brilliant Pebbles, instant reaction response to a Chinese or Russian nuclear missile attack, which is technically do-able under the satellite cyber-weapons concept, is one put forward by the liberals in Congress, in the Pentagon, and in the Bush Administration. They are pushing a so-called new strategy to develop precision guided, but only conventionally armed missiles, supposedly capable of hitting targets anywhere in the world. This idea seems to be on the liberal's menu since Congress, earlier this year, blocked plans to arm our Trident submarine missiles with conventional warheads."

"Chairman Hu must have complained," the partner chuckled.

"Each one would cost one hundred million dollars," Kurt complained. "Think of how many F-22's could be brought on line with the same money."

Kurt continued, "This position also could describe the Democrat presidential candidate's way of thinking. He says he wants to eliminate nuclear weapons, and therefore, would be agreeable to some form of a precision guided type missile system as a non-nuclear strategy. The Defense Department's Undersecretary, who is working on this strategy for the Bush Administration, unfortunately, thinks the concept is also good. He says that attack missiles can be produced which will react to enemy missile attack launch sites, weapons of mass destruction facilities, or on individual terrorist sites, anywhere on earth, and in an hour's time."

"That would be about a half hour too late," the partner commented, sadly, shaking his head.

"The Defense Deputy also says such a system would need good command authority, and also good intelligence to make it work," Kurt continued. "He suggested that the US Strategic Command would be a good command structure," adding, "I can't believe this thinking. Kurt muttered, "This is what we do. For such a system to be viable, the Command generals and admirals would have to man this new computer system twenty-four hours a day. It obviously, on its face, cannot work. This is protecting America on pure luck. The basic nuclear safety of America, would be at an unreasonable risk."

Kurt continued, "The deaths and casualties in such a calamity could involve millions of Americans."

The partner nodded in agreement, standing, intent on a reenergizing rest break, said, "Some guy, in pointing out absolute stupidity, said, 'When someone gets run over by a car going one way, it is no remedy to let the car go back over him in the opposite direction.'"

Kurt grinned, but then paled that such could be a US Defense policy.

CHAPTER XIV
THE OBITUARY

A beautiful Colorado Friday morning, however this July 18, 2008 revealed Review Expert Kurt sitting sullenly before his bank of computers, watching for any enemy missile activity which might become a US problem, and thinking, *"I could see it all happening, and there is absolutely nothing I could do about it. I don/'t have any way of dispatching a protective defensive missile, in time to counteract any enemy missile."*

As Kurt was reflecting on this realistic missile scenario, he heard a noise behind him, someone was trying to whistle the Stars and Stripes Forever, the inspiring march of John Phillip Sousa. The whistle sounds were mostly the passage of a lot air through someone's lips, but the march, while somewhat recognizable, was not a vivid rendition.

"That you partner?" Kurt intoned.

Kurt's partner at Cheyenne Mountain who was just getting back from his leave, and returning to man his computer post, replied, "How did you know it was me?" laughing.

"The Stars and Stripes gave you away," Kurt responded. "I knew it could not be Blitz because he cannot sing, or whistle, anything," adding, "I also knew that you like to try to whistle tunes from time to time. If I had not heard your feeble whistle attempts a few times before, I might not have recognized it," chuckling.

"What did you expect," the partner interposed, "the US Air Force Marching Band?"

Trying to change the subject, Kurt responded, "Welcome back. How was the furlough? How are the folks in St. Louis?"

"Everyone's fine," the still mad partner replied, "but I really am glad to get back to my little cubbyhole here in Cheyenne Mountain," adding, "St. Louis is not the gracious same place I grew up in. Most of my kin are still there, but the people seem different. The streets, particularly at night, are not the same. In fact, in my parents' neighborhood all the old folks either have died, or moved out. Nobody knows one another, or trusts one another anymore."

The partner continued, "My Dad laments about these basic changes, not only in St. Louis, but also all over, especially in the many big cities in America," adding, "He laid this change at the feet of the US loss of its good old fashioned friend, common sense. A transparent thing, which every American community usually could without thinking, count on," adding, "In fact, my Dad handed me 'Common Sense's' obituary," laughing, "I don't know where he got it, or who wrote it. It's called an Obituary of an Old Friend, and I'm going to read it to you, whether you want to listen or not."

"The last thing I need is to listen to an obituary," Kurt laughed, as his partner began quoting.

"We are mourning the loss of an old friend. His name was Common Sense. He died in his adopted land, America, wasting away after a long period of abuse and disinterest.

"Common Sense had devoted his entire life to helping American folks get the job done in schools, hospitals, homes, factories, and even in the courts.

"He gave us such longtime valued lessons, as, when to come in out of the rain; the way the early bird gets the worm; and life is not always fair. He also told us, 'Don't spend more than you earn; adults are in charge here, not the kids; and its okay to come in second, every once in a while.'"

Kurt interjected, now highly interested, "Did you say your Dad wrote this beauty?"

"No," answered the partner. "He would not say who put it together," as he continued reading.

"Common Sense's health, unfortunately, started to decline when he became infected with, 'I'm not responsible for my own actions', along with an 'it's alright if it feels good' virus. This virus got worse as he found he was not able to tell a parent that his child was being given, in school, certain mind altering drugs, all in the name of mental health, or being issued birth control pills, all in the name of protection and sexual freedom. However, he did have to get these same parents' consent to give this same child a common aspirin."

"Or," Kurt snarled, breaking into the recitation, "that carbon dioxide, CO_2, the gas that God gave us to keep our planet livable, to shield us from all the hostile rays coming in from outer space, and to provide the nourishment to our trees and plants, is somehow actually bad, and human caused, and that government should, brainlessly, try to destroy it."

The partner nodded, and continued, "Common Sense seemed to lose his will to live when he was told the God given Ten Commandments were, in fact, contraband and prejudicial; when he saw priests molesting young boys; when he observed an American president accepting campaign loans from a foreign leader in exchange for security related technology given to this same hostile nation; when he saw a jury award millions to a lady who had personally picked up an obvious hot cup of coffee, and then carelessly spilled it on her body, pleading, 'She did not know it was hot.'

"Common Sense came very close to falling into a coma when told that almost a third of American babies are legally murdered just before birth, by US medical authorities, claiming it is a personal right, not, however, found in the Bible, or in the US Constitution.

"Common Sense was caused to drift in and out of consciousness, however, when informed America must offer up the lives of its soldiers, and empty its Treasury in the support, and protection of a certain Middle East nation, by invading and then occupying an adjacent Islamic nation, by then defending the Moslem's anti-Christian beliefs by the purposeful denigration, and destruction of that nation's, and America's own Christianity.

"Common Sense was fatally stricken with cardiac arrest, when informed his services were no longer needed, as the US Government was assuming his various duties, and what he had previously provided, was old fashioned.

"Common Sense died, but not peacefully."

Thinking the verse was finished, Kurt intoned, "I like it. Could you make me a copy?"

"Wait," the partner replied, "There is one last paragraph," then reciting, "Common Sense was preceded in death by his mother, Truth, and his father, Trust; his daughter, Responsibility, and two sons, Diligence and Reason."

"Wonderful close," Kurt exclaimed, "Such truths, such terrible truths."

There was little conversation the rest of that shift, between Kurt and the partner. The simple truths of the 'obituary' kept working on their minds.

It was a week later that Kurt's shift finally put him in line to be off on a Saturday, July 26th, and also a Sunday, July 27, 2008.

He immediately made arrangements to spend time with his lady friend in Colorado Springs.

She, conveniently, invited Kurt for an at-home, Saturday evening dinner, but conditioned it on Kurt taking her to church the next morning.

Kurt readily agreed, telling his lady friend, "I don't go to church too often, but I am a member in good standing of the local, Missouri Synod, Lutheran Church, and they would be elated to see me, and more elated to see you."

The meal was, as usual, super delicious, as Kurt dug into the strawberry cobbler, and sipped on a fresh cup of coffee. It was the pleasant wind up to a beautiful, relaxing day with his lady friend.

Kurt wondered why she continued putting up with him. He would seem to ignore her for several weeks at a time.

She realized he was committed to a very responsible job, and now, as a qualified satellite expert, he would probably be even more busy, and distant.

"Tell me why a church cannot preach either a sermon, or participate in a handout that supports a particular political candidate," the lady friend interposed.

Kurt surprised by the unexpected question, looked at her, saying, "How did that come up, particularly right now?"

She smiled, and replied, "We are going to church tomorrow, and its something that weighed on my mind. We have an election in November."

Kurt finished his dessert, put down his fork, and declared, "As a matter of fact, that very question came up in my church in Seattle a couple of years ago, and I researched its far reaching, unconstitutional prohibitions."

The lady smiled, saying, "I knew you knew the answer."

"I don't know the answer," Kurt responded, "but I can tell you what happened, and how easy it is to take away from Americans, something as basic as merely talking politics in your own church."

"Tell me how it happened?" insisted his hostess.

"It started out as a hot, muggy, ninety-six degree, July 2, 1954 day. The kind that was, in that season, usual in Washington, DC. It coincided with a meeting of a few of the Senate members of the important Finance Committee. Their ranks were greatly depleted by the steamy, non-air conditioned air. No American who cared about what was to happen was watching."

Kurt took a swallow of coffee, and then continued, "Lyndon Baynes Johnson, the Senator from Texas, who many accused of stealing the necessary votes for his initial election, had been re-elected in 1952. During that election, LBJ was accused by some organization that had religious affiliations of being soft on communism. The criticism was free and fair, and true. It got LBJ mad at preachers, however, steaming mad."

Kurt drank some more coffee and continued, "Two anti-Christian, non-profit groups developed an amendment supported by their home state Democrat Senators. One organization was called Facts Forum, and the other was called Committee for Constitutional Government. They pushed their Senators to offer the following anti-church amendment to the pending Senate Tax Bill, then being considered by the Committee. The amendment was worded, 'All non-profits, and all churches, endorsing, or opposing candidates for political office would,' if they did so, 'lose their tax exempt status.'

"Lyndon Johnson, when he looked at this so-called amendment," Kurt muttered, "big, shiny lights grew in his eyes, and he readily agreed to support it. LBJ is quoted as saying, 'I have discussed the matter with the Chairman of the Committee, the Minority Ranking Member of the Committee, and several other members of the Committee, and I understand that the amendment is acceptable to them.'

"LBJ then told the few other members of the Committee who were sweating it out in the steamy meeting room, 'I hope the Chairman will take it to Conference, and that it will be included in the final Bill which Congress passes.' Thus ended the saga."

"You mean that all there is to it?" questioned his lady friend.

"That's all you see publicly, all that's recorded," Kurt responded. "What we don't see is the following. First of all, this is a spending Bill, and it has to start in the House. The House was fully controlled by LBJ's good buddy, and fellow Texan, Democrat Speaker, Sam Rayburn. Sam could easily have gotten rid of this amendment merely by a telephone call," adding, "As a spending Bill, it must already have passed the House, and then be submitted to the Senate. After a Bill has been approved by the Senate, it usually goes to a Conference, to grind out the difference. This still exists in congressional rules."

Kurt stopped momentarily, for another swig of coffee, commenting, "To get to Conference, the Bill, with the attached anti-church amendment, must have somehow passed the Senate," adding, "I looked it up. I found the amendment was included in the final Senate Bill."

Kurt looked at his lady friend, "Remember, LBJ said he had talked to the ranking Minority Committee member. This person had to be a Republican. And that he agreed with the amendment. If that is so, the Republican Party has a duty to answer why their committeeman did not object. It would have thrown out the amendment."

His hostess shook her head in extreme annoyance at this disclosure, as Kurt continued, "The congressional record does show that the Bill was passed by a voice vote, and with the amendment neither unchanged in wording, nor without debate or analysis. There is no written record, and therefore, we have no public record of who supported it."

He continued, "The House Bill version, and the Senate version, thus was sent to Conference. Here it is supposedly reviewed by both political parties, who are represented by appointments to the Conference by party leaders. They always appoint their most trusted political friends, so the leaders can still control what happens."

Kurt finished his coffee, concluding, "So that is how Lyndon Baynes Johnson, later voted by his colleagues their Senate Majority Leader, and then, as Vice President, succeeded to the American presidency, felt about American churches, pastors, and, we can assume, religion in general. He had, like a Lucifer, exacted his payback. Overnight LBJ had, by the wave of his hand, taken away our long cherished, free speech in the pulpit by our Christian American pastors. If this amendment had been in effect prior to the American Revolution, there would have been no revolution. It was the Christian pastors, expounding from their pulpits, which gave it its drive."

His lady friend looked sadly at Kurt, but said nothing and began cleaning up the dirty dishes.

Kurt, leaving for the night, told her he would pick her up at 9:00 a.m. the following morning for church.

She nodded her assent, and as she was closing her front door, intoned to Kurt, "I can't believe it was done so easily. Where were the Republicans we voted for who were always telling us 'Don't worry'? As a matter of fact, where are the Republicans now? Why haven't they repealed that amendment? They have controlled Congress for several years."

Kurt shrugged, "That's a good question."

Kurt arrived at the same door precisely at 9:00 a.m., on Sunday. As they made their way to Kurt's Missouri Synod, Lutheran Church, she told him of her concern about the tendencies of the modern family to by-pass church. That church was becoming increasingly decadent, and irrelevant. That Americans seem, more and more, anxious only to prefer quick and one-sided fixes.

Kurt nodded, and commented, "I agree, and what you say is absolutely true. But then I sit down and tell myself, 'What we are observing is not the end of the world. It is not the end of America. Remember God is still in control.'"

"I wish I had your confidence," his lady friend interposed. "America and its churched seem to dwell on mostly un-Christian things, irrelevant to the usual Bible driven agendas."

"Today's churches are, in some cases, decadent. It is, however, usually in the older denominations. There continue to be problems with homosexuals, and with other un-Christly programs," Kurt admitted. "But remember, God is in control," adding, "Look around you. There are many problems, but Americans, at this point, can still speak freely, can ignore and turn off the media driven, anti-Christian onslaught. They still have their brains, their initiatives, their stick-to-it-tiveness, and above all, their love of family. They can still go to the church that they want, or, if unsatisfied, they can create their own church at home."

They had, by then, reached Kurt's church. As they entered both were heartily greeted by an elated pastor, not expecting to see Kurt, let alone his lady.

As they sat side-by-side alone in their pew, she whispered, "What did you mean about a church at home?"

"Let me tell you a story about a similar Christian problem that took place in Europe," Kurt interposed. "It brought about a world shaking event, the advent of Lutheran founder, Martin Luther. He was a former Catholic priest who, in his day, decried the crumbling Catholic Church, and the decadence of Christianity, in general."

Kurt looked around, to assure himself their conversation was not bothering their neighbors, and continued, "Luther was called on to visit the Christian clergy and churches in Saxony. His reaction was, 'Mercy! Good God! What manifold misery I behold. The common people have no knowledge whatever of Christian doctrine, and alas, many pastors are altogether incapable and incompetent to teach.'

"His answer to the problem, he found, was to prepare a simple Christian catechism. He put it in a simple booklet form. It did not address the pastor, or the teacher. It was aimed solely at only one individual, the Head of the Family."

His lady smiled at this description, and urged him to continue, saying, "The head of the Family is also a big modern problem."

"Each section of Luther's catechism included instructions for the Head of the Family to lead in daily prayers," Kurt continued. "To work, however, it needed not only a family head, but also a family table, or something that brought the family together."

He continued, "The reading of this catechism, or something like it, akin to the old fashioned family Bible hour, could easily be done, right in your own home. It could provide regular interruptions to the modern rat race. To do so, however, requires faith," adding, "For example, Luther's child's bedtime prayer, saying, simply, 'I thank Thee, my Heavenly Father, through Jesus Christ, Thy dear Son - - - I pray

Thee to forgive all my sins - - - Let Thy Holy angel be with me, that the wicked foe may have no power over me. Amen.'"

"What if there is no male head of the family?" the lady questioned.

"There will be," Kurt replied. "It forces a husband, like it or not, to be responsible for the spiritual well being of his family. He has the duty to find that family table."

"It sounds so easy," she whispered. "Can it really be that simple?"

"It requires faith," Kurt concluded, as the choir began the service, adding, "Remember Christ's words in John, 'God so loved the world that he caused His only Son to die for us, that everyone who believes,' the sole price of God's admission to Heaven, will assure that 'we will not die – but have eternal life.'"

Kurt reached for the Hymn book in front of him, admonishing, "Remember, God is in control."

CHAPTER XV
TRADITIONALISTS

The next six months flew by. They went, almost, without Kurt realizing it. While he was fully aware that events were occurring, such as the election of the Democrat candidate for president, on November 4, 2008, and of all the media frenzy surrounding it, it was as though Kurt was suspended in space, and not part of the continuing worldly happenings.

His partner noticed this unusual behavior, and chalked it up to the usual, too much computer gazing. He too had experienced the same from time to time.

Kurt and Blitz contacted one another regularly each month as they had agreed. Their cell phone talks were mostly social as both had agreed to hold up on submitting any of Kurt's continuing fighter plane designs. As a consequence, they were piling up in Kurt's briefcase. Both continued to worry about too much corporate closeness with Chairman Hu's many security stealers. Blitz also remained busy in his troubleshooting capacity. He had been sent all over the nation by his grateful-to-have-him commanding officer, to help alleviate special Air Force problems. However, fifty percent of his time was still spent performing as the main test pilot for the XXII advanced stealth fighter plane, being continually put together at Bowing. He was also testing a new air-to-air missile, which would be part of the XXII's armament.

When they had last talked at the end of November, Blitz related, "I had been highly recommended to be promoted by my CO to a

Brigadier. Several Air Force generals joined in the recommendation. It, however, got put on hold by the power at the Pentagon. Then after several weeks, it was denied, without comment," laughing, adding, "Actually, I would rather stay a Bird Colonel anyway. It commands more respect, and I have much more testing freedom."

"The liberals must have been watching for it," Kurt replied, "after the scorching testimony you gave them."

"The XXII is still the best," ignoring Kurt's comments, Blitz responded. "I would rather be testing that plane, than be promoted out of a job I love," adding, "I just wish I was able to submit to the engineers some of your latest designs, but we better wait. I do, however, want to let you know that I'm testing a new air-to-air missile, and it is super. It could be redeveloped into something that might please you."

Blitz noticed, asking, "Is something amiss with you? You sound unusually sad. Is the Mountain getting to you?" chuckling. "Why don't you take a couple weeks furlough? Go see your folks, and talk to your old neighbors," adding, "You will be surprised at what talking American for a few days will do for you."

Kurt, eager to resume his usual eagerness, took Blitz's sage advice. He arranged for a three week leave, starting the first part of December, clearing it with his fellow review experts, and also with the remaining command at Cheyenne Mountain.

December 23, 2008, a nice sunny day, found Kurt disembarking from the two-prop interim airline airplane that serviced Colorado Springs. To his elation, his lady friend could be seen, just beyond the gate barriers, smiling, and waving toward him.

It was the first time each had an opportunity to run toward the other. They clasped one another in a bear hug that registered, for the first time, each ones growing affection for the other.

"How was home?" she asked. "How were the folks?"

"Fine. Fine," Kurt replied, chuckling. "Blitz should hang out his psychiatric shingle. Home for a few days, plus you, was exactly what I needed."

Kurt continued, "Thanks for meeting me. I thought with school Christmas vacation, and other commitments, you would be home with your folks."

"I did spend a few days," she answered, "but I had good reasons to come back to Colorado Springs. I have a surprise for you," smiling, and grabbing Kurt's shoulder.

Kurt looked at her, surprise in his face, asking, "What is this all about?"

"When you took me to your church last summer," she explained, "I was so impressed with it, I decided to join. I have now finished all the church's instructions, and the pastor told me when he found out you would be back, that he would bring me into the church, tonight, as part of their special Christmas program."

"Wow, that is a surprise," Kurt admitted.

"And the angel said unto her, fear not, Mary, for thou hast found favor with God," could be heard as part of Kurt's church's Christmas program on that 23rd of December evening. Kurt watched from his church pew, with pride, as his lady friend stood in the front of the church with another new inductee.

"He shall be great, and shall be called Son of the Highest," the Christmas recitation continued, along with the pastor's rote wording admitting new church members, "Shepherds abiding in the field - - - the angel of the Lord came upon them - - - said unto them - - - Fear not: for, behold, I bring you good tidings of great joy, which shall be to all people - - - born this day - - - a Savior, which is Christ the Lord."

Kurt listened intently, as his preacher finished his bringing in words, and began the part where new inductees would swear allegiance - - - "And they came with haste, and found Mary and Joseph and the baby lying in a manger."

The pastor, and the ongoing Christmas story of Christ's birth, concluded its part, as Kurt's lady friend had now become the church's newest member.

Kurt stood in his pew as she made her way along the aisle to him, and, smiling, sat beside him for the remainder of the service.

Following the church doings, Kurt told his lady friend, "I have a surprise for you."

Without waiting for her response, he interposed, "I have made late dinner reservations for us at the most expensive restaurant in town, in honor of your new church affiliation."

"Thank you," she answered, and then suggested, "Don't you think a congratulatory kiss would be in order?" smiling.

Leaning over toward her, in the pew, oblivious to all the churchly things going on around them, Kurt planted a lingering kiss on the lips of his lady friend. The action evoked several smiles from those nearby.

Following evening church, and following their lingering dinner at the costliest restaurant in town, Kurt muttered, "I like the food you serve much better."

"How's school?" Kurt commented, as the couple started to make their way back over the twenty miles between the restaurant and Mary's Colorado Springs apartment home, adding, "You teach seventh grade in a public elementary school, don't you?"

"I teach English and American History to a class of seventh graders," she replied. "It is a public school located in an area where most of my pupils come from working class homes, although I do have a sprinkling of Air Force kids, plus a few from families whose parents are teachers in the local college."

"How are they doing?" Kurt asked. "How are you doing?" Are you able to use the History and English texts you want?"

"Some students are doing well," Mary responded. "They are the ones who get good support at home. Most, however, like the national SAT scores prove, are not doing so well," adding, "I always use references to History and English textbooks located in the Public Library to supplement my courses. These give my students a more Americanized feature to History. These explain, and expand, on the Constitution, and also identify the American image. They tell the students about George Washington, being a major factor in the history of America, along with the histories of the other founding fathers."

"Do the parents give you any trouble about that?" Kurt asked.

"Not really the parents," Mary replied. "Most of the static comes from the other teachers. They, in turn, are pushed by the local Education Association, who complains I make my students work too hard," adding, "Most of the seventh graders know I make them work hard, and therefore, the ones that don't want to work, opt out of my class, and into the other two History classes. That is fine with me, because I get the students who want to learn."

Kurt laughed, saying, "That is a good way to do things. I'll have to tell Blitz of your plan of battle, and how well it works," adding, "You mentioned the SAT scores. What do they show?"

"For the years 2007 and 2008, the most recent high school graduating classes, remained at the lowest level in a decade. Out of a possible eight hundred points on just the Math section, the average was only four hundred ninety-four. The History and English averages were even worse. I like to think my students improved on the averages a little. I know my students should have done well, because we talked about some of the same questions as part of our normal class work."

She continued, "The thing that bothers me most, however, is not the SAT scores, but it is the tendency of modern students to plagiarize. They increasingly are using things they find on the internet. Thirty-six percent readily admitted they did so. The bigger problem is that they did not think it was wrong. In fact, ninety-three percent of the same students claimed they were satisfied with these ethics."

"Whatever feels good, huh?" Kurt echoed. "Shades of liberal TV."

He continued, "It is a never ending battle between what I call American traditionalists, and American radicals," adding, "Traditionalists stress America's long dependence on the achievements of previous generations. This is compared with the radicals, who depend on, and turn their back on, American History. They urge their own visions, which benefit only them, and bear no resemblance to actual American experience."

"That is an unusual way of describing it," Mary replied, "but it is true."

"Society, basically, lives on its vision of previous American existence, built on facts that habitually have happened before," Kurt continued. "Traditionalists have deep down, abiding roots and ideas about what we are all about. We constantly form hopes for ourselves, and for our families, and our grandchildren, based on what we know has occurred before. This attitude sets up our agenda in both out social and also our political lives. These lasting roots stay the same for generation after generation," adding, "If you think about it, the power to shape and control the minds and imaginations of others is the most powerful force in the world."

Kurt continued, "What motivates most Americans most, is not

the state of the economy. It is who is nominated for an Emmy, or some such other immaterial thing. These trivialities are developed in the minds of the radicals, who have emerged to set the tone in the arts, the movies, the entertainment industry, the publishing houses, the TV media, and the press. When these people pull together with an underlying purpose, in the same direction, they can do much, and lasting harm to out traditionalist culture."

"Television programs, movies, and even music," Kurt continued expounding, "are extremely effective, if they constantly push the same ideological slants, attacking our culture in the way that the radicals want. Since a great many of Americans choose these modes as their entertainment, eventually the slants will effectively inculcate the biases, and provide the changes that the radicals want," adding, "It is the TV producers, directors, and editors, who decide what news should be covered, and how it is to be depicted. Radical scriptwriters make the decisions as to what behaviors shall be acclaimed, and what dissed; what matters are to be taken seriously, and those not; what to laugh at, and who to sneer at. Publishers decide what subjects are to be printed, and what books are hidden from the American public. So-called radical critics control how we feel about plays, and music."

"I had really not thought about those aspects at all," Mary admitted.

"It is in the academic fields," Kurt continued. "All the way from Philosophy to History to English to Political Science and Psychology, where the radical trendsetters have had a heyday, and allowed several years to manipulate the moral, Christian, and spiritual values, and core of our American traditions. They have been chipping away at them since these same people were, in their beginning, campus radicals, disrupting our traditional society back in the 1960's. These revolutionists are now tenured professors, department chairs, deans, and presidents of many prestigious colleges and universities. The radicals did not have to leave campus, but persuaded friendly liberal cohorts in the university system to hire them as faculty. Like a snake, the radicals have coiled around the power of academia."

"That's true," Mary commented.

Kurt continued, "The radicals now set the curriculum and hire the new faculty. They decide the textbooks, and which professional writings are to be accepted by the academic journals. They are the ones who, in fact, have designed your SAT tests," adding, "They also are the ones who teach, and certify, your local History and English high school teachers," laughing, "Mary excepted."

"That is all perfectly true," Mary again admitted, "and while I saw it going on around me, I never associated the phenomenon with people like me personally. It now seems perfectly clear the reason that education has declined at an alarming rate, and at every level. The US morality factor, obviously, has also been denigrated in our families, the churches, and in individuals. The movies, television, the press, the music, the novels, and the videos constantly depict attitudes and behaviors that would have shocked my grandparents, and even my parents, when I was growing up."

The couple had now reached Mary's neighborhood, and she asked Kurt, as their conversation from then on would be limited, "What can we do about it?"

"It is difficult to reverse such an imaginative and intellectual momentum. The radicals are aware of this, and have caught us off guard," Kurt pondered, adding, "First, we need more teachers to do what you are doing. Assign older texts, as supplements, from local libraries to give the students a true look at history."

Kurt continued, "Our Christian churches are going to have to be our savior, but the radicals have constantly attacked our religious institutions relentlessly," adding, "They have un-Christianized many of them, but there are sufficient born again Christians to carry the day, if they unite," adding, "I am not going to admit radical dominance or inevitability. If we find traditional Americans of equal commitment and creativity, and be patient, plus keep our faith in God and Christ, we can prevail. We can dispatch these radicals. Americans, or most of them, are still a unique people."

They had reached Mary's apartment now, and as Kurt escorted her toward her door in the now pitch-black night, Mary told him, "There was a nineteenth century, well known German philosopher. He was an atheist. He said, 'Western civilization is based on Christianity, and if we wanted to destroy that Western civilization, all anyone has to do is destroy and remove Christianity.' I think his name was Friedrich

Nietzsche," suddenly noticing a blazing star, which caused her to comment, "Look, an angel," laughing.

"Your own special angel," Kurt told her, giving Mary a good night kiss at her door.

CHAPTER XVI
THE APPOINTMENTS

On a gloomy February 28, 2009, an off day Saturday, Kurt, using his cell phone, contacted Blitz for their monthly contact.

"Where are you?" Kurt asked, when Blitz finally answered.

"I'm sitting in an absolutely gorgeous fighter air plane called the XXII, sitting on the outskirts of Seattle, and sitting in one of the Bowing test areas," Blitz replied, laughing. "What's new?"

"Wish I was with you," Kurt responded. "Getting bored again here," adding, "Thought I would ask you your thoughts on President Obama, now, after his first two months."

"You caught me at a good time," Blitz replied, "the tower just told me I will be sitting here for a good half hour. Put up your feet, relax, and lets talk politics," laughing.

Blitz echoed, "What do I think about Obama's appointments? That's a good question. Some are not so bad. Some are atrocious," adding, "My main interest is in his appointments to the Defense Department positions, and to the Intelligence posts."

"Who are some of the 'not so bad' appointments?" Kurt asked.

"The guy Obama picked to be the Director of National Intelligence, is better than most," Blitz responded. "You remember him, retired Admiral Dennis C. Blair, don't you? He is the very same Admiral the liberal congressman complained about at our hearings last summer. He was once the head of the Institute for Defense Analysis, and, in that position, made a strong recommendation for US unlimited production of the F-22."

"Oh yeah," Kurt muttered. "Now I remember. As Director of National Intelligence, what does he do? What does he control?"

"As I understand it," Blitz replied, "Blair would be responsible for setting objectives and also standards, for sixteen of the now separated, and dangerously spread out intelligent groups. They are almost not recognizable as intelligence agencies. I'm talking about the so-called CIA, the Defense Intelligence Agency, the National Security Agency, and the others."

"I had forgotten all these other various groups still existed," Kurt admitted. "To bring them under control could be like trying to manage, out of control, independent minded mules, then trying to close the barn door after these mules are already out."

Chuckling, Blitz intoned, "Could be a problem. Let me tell you what my CO told me about this retired Admiral Blair."

Blitz continuing, "Blair was head of the Pacific Command, boss from 1999-2002, with headquarters in Honolulu. This is America's largest military command. It is composed of some two hundred thousand people, and includes the US West Coast, and extends all the way to the East Coast of Africa."

"After he took command," Blitz continued, "And this fact should interest you, he thoroughly reviewed the Command's then existing war plans. Blair did not like them, or agree with them, particularly as they dealt with a military confrontation with Red China."

Kurt's eyes lit up with that disclosure, asking, "What did he do?"

"He ordered the Command's whole staff in Honolulu to throw out the old, and give him some new, more realistic, more aggressive, war plans," Blitz countered, adding, "It was a laborious job for the 'used to not working' staff, taking thousands of man hours to complete. The staff called it the 'Blair Witch Project'," chuckling.

"Sounds promising," Kurt intoned.

"Blair," Blitz continued, "as Director of National Intelligence, will also have jurisdiction over the US security groups in US Forces in Japan, Korea, and Alaska, and all special operations," adding, "The big thing is he will have control over the usually out-of-control CIA. This will be a major challenge."

"Remember," Kurt replied, "Obama is still boss. What happens will be what he dictates."

"Maybe so, maybe not," Blitz responded. "Admiral Blair, according to my CO, can make himself well understood. While Blair was commander in the Pacific, he had a face-to-face meeting with a Red Chinese Admiral who was dissing Blair on his attitude regarding Taiwan. My CO told me Blair looked the Chinese admiral in the eye, and told him, 'Admiral, let me tell you a couple of things. First, I own the water out there,' he was pointing to the Pacific Ocean visible to both through a window, and, 'Second, I own the sky over the water out there. Now don't you think we should talk about something more constructive?'"

"Wow. I like that," Kurt responded.

"One more story about Retired Admiral Blair," Blitz declared, "This tells me a lot about the man. While he was known as a hard taskmaster, and he himself known as a workaholic, he did have his light moments. Several years ago, Blair became the captain of an American destroyer, by the name of Cochrane, which called Japan as its home port. His crew had been at sea for many weeks, and Blair found they were getting uneasy, so he devised a sure way to entertain them. Blair decided he was going to water ski behind the destroyer. Going over the side, he was fed a rope by a supporting gig. He got all set up behind the coasting destroyer, ready to go. The engine room was signaled full speed ahead. Not designed for skiers, the powerful boat gave him a powerful upward surge, and the Admiral was pulled head over tea kettle into the sea, much to the glee and delight of all the sailors gathered on the fantail."

Kurt let loose with an involuntary belly laugh, exclaiming, "I like this guy. I hope he works out."

Kurt continued, "Anyone else you like?"

"Not too many," Blitz replied. "However, there is a guy by the name of William J. Lynn, III, who is supposed to be appointed to the important Number Two position in the Defense Department."

"With a name like that, he must be descended from royalty," Kurt joked.

"The engineers at Bowing tell me he is better than most," Blitz responded. "He is the Senior Vice President for Government Operations at Raytheon Company, one of our best defense contractors."

"That sounds good," Kurt agreed.

"The liberals, however, complain that Lynn has recently lobbied their Defense Appropriation Committee, asking them to buy missiles, sensors, radar, and a series of advanced technology, and intelligence programs developed by Raytheon."

"This guy sounds even better," Kurt answered. "I hope he has America's interests as his first priority."

Kurt then interposed, "Remember a few months ago when the Air Force was proposing that 'Cyber Command' was important enough to be established as an Air Force major command, alongside the other Air Force commands?"

"If I remember correctly," Blitz asserted, "Cheyenne Mountain was also to be Cyber Command's headquarters."

"It was reported in the Pentagon's *Armed Forces News Service* last fall," Kurt asserted. "The Mountain CO told me that there was ordered a big gathering of high ranking Air Force brass. It took place somewhere in Colorado. The generals were told, on orders from Secretary Gates himself, who, using the excuse of nuclear bomb handling negligence, that, not only was there not going to be an independent Cyber Command, but that the present cyber operations would be further reduced to only a numbered, Air Force component, a step down from a major command, in Air Force organizational terms."

"That does not make sense," Blitz responded. "The Air Force has always wanted a Cyber Command."

"The general who is now running it, according to my CO, says that cyber warfare efforts will be considerably scaled back, if not abolished, and its staff will now be allocated into a new Air Force Nuclear Command instead," adding, "The new general is quoted as saying, 'The new command will bring together all of our US nuclear weaponry under one leadership. The new command, however, will only be a numbered component, a force provider to the Air Force, but only within the Air Force Space Command."

"That description is how we used to designate a Bomber Wing in the Air Combat Command," Blitz complained. "That is stupid, stupid."

"The General also is quoted by my CO as saying, 'Space Command is already the repository of the technical and engineering expertise required.' This big change is really to counteract a perceived big power grab by some generals to control the proposed Space Command," Kurt admitted. "In fact, my CO told me about a former National Cyber Security Division Director, in the Department of Homeland Security. He complained that the Air Force generals were summarily overruled by the civilian leadership not only in the Defense, but in other departments. Several other US Defense experts were shocked at the change, saying it is vital that the US must address the issue of cyber warfare. It cannot ignore it, or leave such an important defense hanging in the air."

"It looks like Chairman Hu rides again," Blitz commented. "The security of our America is still in the hands of incompetents, and those who are willing to trade their country's sovereignty, and, indeed, its very survival, for money in their bank account, lavishly provided by Red China."

"Right," echoed Kurt, adding, "However, not withstanding his good choices, our new president has seen fit to appoint some very troubling people to very important positions dealing with arms control."

"Who are you talking about?" Blitz asked.

"For one, a guy by the name of Robert J. Einhorn is asking to be approved as an Undersecretary of State, specifically for Arms Control and International Security. Einhorn is currently part of the Center for Strategic and International Studies. Before that, he worked for the Clinton Presidency, specializing in non-proliferation policies. In 2003, he criticized Republican-China policies of Bush II for imposing numerous economic sanctions on Red China, when Chairman Hu openly sold arms to various rogue states, contending the better way was to talk to China."

Laughing, Blitz countered, "I don't remember any Bush economic impositions. All I remember is that both the Clinton and the Bush II Red China policies led to grand scale larceny, compromises on US security and technology."

"The second appointment problem," Kurt continued, "Is a man by the name of Vann H. Van Diepen, who now is part of the National Intelligence Council, a liberal, non-profit group. He is well known for opposing any sanctions on Red China. He supposedly spent fourteen years as a State Department Arms Control official. All during that time, he was known to be against stopping Red China from anything."

"What is his job to be?" Blitz asked.

"Van Diepen is supposed to get Einhorn's old job as the Assistant Undersecretary of State for Non-proliferation."

"Same old game of Musical Chairs," Blitz muttered. "Same game. Same chairs. Same people. Same liberal, anti-American ideas, and Chairman Hu always wins."

"It is also the same old stuff we get, and got, from Mario Mancuso, Bush's Undersecretary of Commerce for Industry and Security," Kurt muttered disgustedly. "The same attitude was prevalent, and evident, when the money makers, in promoting their so-called Validated End-User Program with China, a fantasy designed to give China access to much of our technical matters, for supposed commercial use only, on the unverified promise China would not use it for military matters. Further, that production using said technology would be accomplished by state owned and operated Red Chinese corporations."

"How much of this crap will the American people continue to believe?" Blitz intoned. "How long will they accept these security risks?" adding, "If they realized the extreme danger to their children and grand-children, they would probably charge, and attack the Congress with drawn pitchforks."

"Yet, Mancuso rattles on, saying, 'The US-China relationship is critical in the prosperity of both countries, and the Commerce Department will continue to consider ways to expand commercial high technology trade with China," Kurt recited.

"Bullshit," Blitz blurted out, almost involuntarily, but stopped from commenting further as he closed out their cell phone conversation, saying, "I was just informed by the tower my runway is cleared. Talk to you in March. Get your pitchfork ready."

CHAPTER XVII
STRING OF PEARLS

The calendar said spring, but the continuing three feet of drifting snow, and the thirty-five mile per hour, northwest wind, would belie that conclusion.

Although it was March 28, 2009, Colorado Springs was experiencing Mother Nature's last ditch winter storm, settling once and for all who was boss.

It was a messy slosh, but if you were cozy and warm inside a mountain, it really didn't make "no never mind" to coin a phrase.

Kurt, oblivious to the storm, was contemplating all sorts of things, sitting alone during his rest break. His avid concentration was, however, abruptly interrupted by the Cheyenne Mountain CO, who, like Miss Muffet, sat down beside him, saying, "I just ran across a late filed report. It was issued about the first of December, by the Norfolk based, US Joint Forces Command. The report is entitled, Joint Operating Environment - 2008. It clearly nominates Red China as the main emerging nation-state, which American armed forces would be confronted by, in any future war situation."

"How come it took so long to get to you?" Kurt asked.

His CO hunched his shoulders with an I-don't-know, saying, "This command, any more, does not get the respect it used to get," adding, "China, being clearly identified as the most significant potential threat to the US, might be the reason. The report lays out Beijing's continuing efforts to manufacture political influence and military power, along with, what is called, its strategic oil shipping route. It extends from the Middle East to China."

"China is why you got it late," Kurt admonished. "Don't you know we cannot speak in anger, or point fingers at our ominous Asian friend Red China?" adding, "What does the report say, even if it is old news?"

"It graphically shows where that Red China is putting together huge numbers of nuclear submarines, along with a simultaneous big buildup in other ships to augment their continuing growing navy," his CO pointed out.

"I read about China's so-called 'String-of-Pearls' strategy," Kurt commented. "Chairman Hu worries about the present enormous, big ship US Navy being able to shut down China's necessary imports of oil, all of which they need in order to keep China's factories greased," adding, "And well they should. Eighty percent of their oil goes through the Straits of Malacea. I'm sure our Navy must have a strategy of closing off those Straits, if necessary, which, with all of our aircraft carriers, we should easily be able to do."

"Don't assume anything," the CO commented, laughing, adding, "The report continues saying that China ships fifteen million barrels of oil each day through the Straits of Malacca, and seventeen million barrels per day through the Strait of Hormuz," adding, "China is evidently establishing a strong military presence all along those shipping lanes. The report further states that their military buildup includes the building of naval bases, creating overland supply routes to China, plus new Chinese only port facilities, a planned canal to be dug traversing Thailand, and two new military bases located in the South China Sea."

"Sounds like a lot of money," Kurt joked. "I hope our State Department, and our Commerce Department, has furnished Chairman Hu with enough cash," laughing.

"Red China is also moving, big time, into the Indian Ocean area, and into southeast Asia, according to the report," the CO continued. "It lists Pakistan's Gwadar Port, situated near the mouth of the Persian Gulf, as a newly created, Red Chinese, naval base, and surveillance platform."

China must get along better with the Pakistanis than we do," Kurt commented.

"The report also talks about the creation of a new Chinese port at Hambantota, Sri Lanka, along with the building of an air field located in nearby Woody Island."

"It amazes me," Kurt offered, "what China is able to do on our money. Of course, they also have a free range to graze in any of our US technology. Anything they want to steal. Oh, excuse me, I meant borrow."

The Cheyenne Mountain CO smiled, knowingly.

Kurt continued, "Even with China's grandiose String of Pearls strategy, along with its attending high cost, the thing that worries me more is China's obviously putting most of its eggs into the development of satellite weapons, along with cyber-warfare capabilities. The US, at least in the short term, with its present military makeup, should be able to combat the most that Chairman Hu can throw, but to adopt and fund cyberspace warfare continued to be a, 'don't want to get involved' American blank."

"The report ends up disclosing that the Chinese are the most significant present threat to the US, and will remain so for the next twenty-five years," the CO continued. "It also warns that the Reds are continuing to monitor, and to study, US military strategy and thinking. The report thinks that the Chinese understand US strengths and weaknesses, better than America understands those of the Chinese."

"Every nation in the world," Kurt complained, "understands America's strengths and weaknesses better than the defense planners in charge at the Pentagon, or many of our so-called intelligent Americans, who don't really think about it."

"What do you mean?" asked his CO.

"For instance," Kurt responded, "last February 8, 2009, our newly elected Vice President, in a speech to the European Security Conference in Munich, delighted the Russians and the Chinese, along with all those in the world who oppose any kind of American missile nuclear defense. The Vice President was quoted, saying, 'The US would continue to develop missile defenses to counter growing worldwide capability, 'provided' the technology is 'proven' to work, and is 'cost effective','" adding, "Our enemies, by those words, were assured that the Democrats were back, and in control with their Luddite views on anti-missile technology. These same enemies, currently spending billions to develop their own modern, nuclear missile systems, were given concrete evidence that the US, now controlled by the same old Democrats', and the same old liberals', stop-by-all-means anti-missile technology, adherents have returned to power, and will not build, or deploy, the very vital satellite missile defense, which America will need to survive.

"Did not these same liberals use the old 'mutually assured destruction' (MAD) strategy, alleging that missile defense would never work, back during the Reagan presidency days," adding, "It is now so obvious that missiles can work, as demonstrated by the Air Forces' recent hitting a bullet with a bullet missile test."

"That is why the Vice President's words 'proven' and 'cost effective' are so important to these same anti-missile technology scums," Kurt muttered. "Now they talk about how a viable missile system can only be deployed if and when it is 'proven' or 'perfected', which they know to be an ever moving impossible goal."

"Another way to fool the American people," the CO noted, "using those words as a never-ending excuse, to be used over and over again, as an explanation to the American people, yet claiming they are actually for missile defense."

"I hope none of these traitors have any grandchildren," Kurt intoned. "They will be the ones who will surely take the brunt of their brainless, anti-missile thinking," adding, "or maybe Chairman Hu has already issued an invitation to them to come live in his beautiful, smog-filled, dictatorial, storm trooper dominated atmosphere."

"One thing is for sure," the CO commented, "such an anti-defense group won't remain alive in America, when and if the people ever find out what these liberals have done to their posterity, along with their sovereignty."

"It does not help matters to have someone like Richard Danzig, a former Bill Clinton Navy Chief Defense Advisor, who held the job of Deputy Secretary of Defense," Kurt commented. "He is also a Yale lawyer, and Rhodes Scholar, who previously served in various posts in the Pentagon under Carter and Bush I. He is a well known liberal, and an anti-missile defense advocate," adding, "He has often, and publicly, stated, 'The US can't do everything by itself. The US must get its allies to assume the burden militarily, and international security problems require the US to use non-military assets.'"

"Did he really say that?" the CO asked. "Is he really slated to be the president's Chief Defense Advisor?" adding, "God help us."

"If Danzig's advice is followed," Kurt continued, "the US may as well surrender," adding, "Also promulgated to work at the Pentagon is Clinton's Chief-of-Staff, John Podesta, now embedded at the ultra liberal Center for American Progress, along with the Center's own Rudy deLeon, who was also Clinton's Undersecretary of Defense for Personnel and Readiness. Rudy continues to advocate more gays in the military, and more women in combat roles. Those two are very likely to be re-appointed to some comparable section of the new administration's Pentagon."

"If the Pentagon is to be run by such liberal national security experts," the CO muttered, "All our military, including the functions and the personnel right here at Cheyenne Mountain will obviously be put on a crash diet. American military men, in the end, will pay for this perfidy with their blood."

"Not only will they lose their blood," Kurt responded, "their children will also lose their country."

He continued, "If American's were truly interested in the truth of the status of our nuclear missile defenses in this increasingly necessary missile age," Kurt commented. "All one would need to do is take a close look at the 'Stimulus Law', that was enacted by the Democrats in the Congress on February 15, 2009."

"Don't forget that it was three Republican Senators that iced it," chuckled the CO.

"I consider them as Democrats," Kurt countered.

He continued, "The President's security policies and programs all as outlined in that Stimulus Law, will have the effect of transforming the US from being the top nation in the world, as they were under Reagan, to, in effect, a nuclear impotency. While at the very same time, the world watches our enemies publicly building up their nuclear capabilities," adding, "It is as you pointed out regarding our other defenses, the American people also really have no idea that such a current state of affairs exists with regard to our US nuclear defense situation."

Kurt continued, "Under Clinton and Bush II, America voluntarily, and stupidly, shot itself in the foot, by supporting a seventeen year, unilateral freeze on its nuclear testing. We could easily have modernized and kept our nuclear stocks in good working order by just a few underground nuclear tests during that time. We had the time, and the place, to easily conduct those tests, and we had the technical personnel who were able to conduct them," adding, "Our leaders, brainlessly, under the spell of the anti-nuclear people, allowed a steady decline to our nuclear weapons, and also in their reliability."

"To allow seventeen years to go by without using the technology available, and not giving our nuclear scientists a chance to practice their trade," the CO commented, "is bound to take its toll," adding, "In fact, I would judge that if you factor in deaths, and retirements, similar technicians would have to be retrained and recreated all over again."

"That is only part of it," Kurt responded. "Those that are still involved as US directors in our remaining nuclear laboratories, the ones who are supposed to keep our leaders posted about the status of our nuclear stockpile, refuse to certify with certainty the status of our nuclear weapons."

Kurt continued, "Since President Reagan's time, America has, in fact, reduced its number of nuclear weapons by about seventy-five percent, when compared to the number that were, or could be deployed, at that time. In fact, under the US-Russian treaty signed by Bush II and Putin, back in 2002, we now have less than the twenty-two hundred fielded nuclear weapons, which were permitted by that pact," adding, "Our new president, never-the-less, wants to cut them back to only five hundred deployed nuclear weapons."

"How do you know this?" asked his CO.

"He said so," Kurt responded. "Also his Office of Management and Budget indicates as confirmed by the Stimulus Law, there will be no modernization of our nuclear stockpile, and no upgrading of the capability to produce new weapons, or to rehabilitate old ones. Our new president has said he will also seek the swift ratification of the Comprehensive Test Ban Treaty, rejected forcefully, and by big margins, by the Senate back in 1997. This would permanently stop all future US nuclear tests. We would be at the mercy of our non-complying enemies, who would be laughing at our foolishness."

"Would the President really do this?" asked the CO. "Would the Congress really approve such a thing?"

"Don't forget," Kurt reminded him, "we now have a Congress that is majority loaded with liberal Democrats," adding, "If they are not enough, the Democrats can always count on the traitorous vote of Senator Spector, if necessary. Also many actions can be accomplished by Executive Order only."

"The unthinking American people," the CO responded, "in effect, could have voted for their own demise," paling.

"Consider the new president's public vow to seek an arms control situation that would, in effect, cripple US defenses even further, by re-applying the terms of the START II Treaty," Kurt related. "Plus, if you combine START limitations with the other nuclear stockpile cuts, the obvious, practical effect is to destroy the American long time strategy of the Triad, which three legs have, in the past, kept our enemies at bay," adding, "Under those new liberal conditions, our nuclear submarines would also have to be taken off 'Hair Trigger' alert status."

"I was kidding before," admitted the CO, "but the majority of American voters, may just have elected to hang themselves."

"It is impossible to verify compliance with our nuclear enemies," Kurt muttered. "We are, voluntarily throwing, all of America into our enemies' ash can."

"It is a dooms day scenario," concluded the CO. "The new President has four years, and with his ability to convince the public with his glib believable lies, maybe another four years. What can we do?"

"We must look again," Kurt offered, "to the same Americans who gave us our Republic, and again, over the years, both in war and in peace, preserved our Republic. Most of all, who also preserved our Christian, nation saving, heritage. Someone said, 'Remember, it was not raining when Noah started building the Ark.'"

CHAPTER XVIII
THE CLINTON LEGACY CODE

April 15, 2009, marked a milestone in Kurt Reitz's uneventful life. He was finally promoted to Major in the US Air Force. He still remained, however, as the same System Review Expert.

While Kurt did only the same necessary computer observing, and completed all the movements he had done before, he had long ago concluded, his job was vitally important. It was just as important as was the job of the President of the United States.

Kurt, in doing his job, of course, discovered no Chinese missiles heading for the US, at present, but he knew his job, and if missiles were to come, Kurt would be the first to know it. He would make sure, so would America. Even so, because of US disarmament advocates, there was no way to stop them.

Mary cooked a special dinner to commemorate the promotional occasion, and Blitz commented, in a telephone congrats, "There must be something special in the hearts of the Air Force Promotion Board to grant this promotion honor, on the same day it confiscates your income tax," laughing.

Kurt and Blitz had religiously kept up their monthly cell phone conversation, but had not personally seen one another for several months.

It was another story, as to Kurt and Mary. Realizing their growing, deep love for one another, their affection finally culminated with Kurt proposing marriage to Mary. The mutual declaration took place, ironically during the Lord's Prayer, as Kurt was inspired by, "Thy will be done," at a 2009 Christmas service at their church. They both agreed, however, to hold up on a wedding ceremony for a few months, until Kurt had completed his service obligations, and had found new employment for his aeronautical engineering prowess.

In the spring of 2010, however, Kurt received an urgent telephone call from Blitz, saying, "I just got a disturbing e-mail from the staff of the conservative, pro-American, nuclear defense Senator from Oklahoma. He complains that, due to the intervention of Obama, the arms control advocates in his unilateral disarmament administration, have taken complete command over the crucial elements in the Pentagon, and in the State Department, and in other agencies concerned with providing a credible US defense. The Senator demands that the defeatist, arms control agenda, which is mistakenly based on their idea that, if the US merely reduces its number of nuclear weapons it will deploy, it will automatically create and cause a more stable and loving world situation, and therefore, diminish the threat of nuclear wars. Further, that nuclear war is so destructive that it is rendered unthinkable."

"If these defeatists prevail," Kurt replied, "it will be our enemies that survive and prevail in this hostile world, while our America will be destroyed," adding, "What did the Senator want you to do?"

"It boils down to the fact," Blitz replied, "that he needs both of us to again provide testimony to his committee, in an attempt to reverse this defeatist attitude, or at least to give the public an idea of what is going on. He hopes Americans will protest in great numbers."

Blitz continued, "The Senator is also very concerned about the Obama Administrations' attempts to quash production of the F-22."

"I thought the Pentagon had made a deal to increase the F-22 numbers to a total of one hundred eighty-three aircraft," Kurt responded.

"At three hundred fifty million dollars each," Blitz replied, "Obama and his disarming liberals are even trying to squash that," adding, "The Senator is setting his hearing dates for us on the same day the Democrat Chairman opens his hearings on Obama's proposed new START Treaty, or June 10, 2010. Shall I tell him you are available?" Can you get off duty for a week?"

"I'll be there," Kurt answered, "if I have to go AWOL."

"Okay," Blitz responded. "You can expect a subpoena to be served on you, soon, to appear, starting June 10th. Let me know when you have been served, and I will arrange to pick you up."

At the earliest time after he and Blitz had hung up, Kurt found reason to contact his CO at Cheyenne Mountain to make sure there would be no problem in getting his leave time on the agreed upon dates.

Kurt explained to his commander that he was being summoned as an expert witness, and needed that particular week of June 10th off. That the CO could also expect a US Marshall would stop by with a subpoena for Kurt.

The CO, upon hearing Kurt, observed, "I would strongly suggest, since you have over sixty days of accumulated leave, that we arrange a two week leave now, before any subpoena gets here. It might be difficult to arrange after the Air Force learns you are going to testify."

"I agree," Kurt acknowledged. "Could you have your staff get it arranged from June 1, 2010 through June 20, 2010? That should cover it," adding, "I don't want the Obama powers-that-be to stop any of my testimony to the Committee, which will ensure they know Chairman Hu is doing everything in his power to put China in a position to unilaterally attack and destroy the US. Plus the indictment that the US government, for the last ten years, has done absolutely nothing to defend America against this coming catastrophe. In fact, they have given Chairman Hu the very ropes with which to hang us."

The CO offered, "Obama people seem to want to be gleefully standing beside Hu, on his gallows, ready to help pull the switch to complete his massacre," adding, "Has our Secretary-of-State, Hillary Clinton, given us any hope of cutting off this love Hu, love China-Obama thing?"

"Are you kidding," Kurt replied. "She is more likely to be a part of Hu's staff. She and Bill Clinton are both still under Hu's thumb. This derives from their actions in 1992, during Bill Clinton's first run for president. They made a devil's pact with the communist Chairman, which was secrets, in exchange for several millions of illegal cash, out of Red China's Treasury, and paid directly into Bill Clinton's campaign chest. The Clintons should hang their eyes in shame, to accommodate these instances of communist larceny, and to allow stealing of much of our vital nuclear, computer, military, and rocket technology. American secrets were, thus, surreptitiously transferred to Red China, and to its military, including all of the US nuclear legacy code. The Clintons' traitorous acts allowed Red China to bypass the several years it would have taken to develop that same nuclear information on their own. It enabled Chairman Hu to be now in a position to attack and destroy America."

"You think he still holds that over them?" the CO asked. "That incident is almost twenty years old."

"Chairman Hu recognizes the grand prize when he see it," laughed Kurt. "But to give you another example, remember back in 2009, Bill Clinton, reluctantly, agreed to mete out to the public some of the hidden donor information about his so-called Clinton Foundation. It was to make sure he and Hillary were not too beholden to such highbrow donors, as kings and princes from Saudi Arabia. Bill, the data revealed, back in 2004, made a uninspired speech to a group who was associated with a non-descript corporation called Accoona. In return for Bill's Speech, his so-called foundation was graciously donated two hundred thousand shares of Accoona stock. To complete this fairy tale, in 2006, the same Clinton foundation sold the same two hundred thousand shares for an unbelievable seven hundred thousand dollars. In 2007, a loss was reported, in data filed by Accoona, in a necessary report to the SEC. They reported to the SEC they had been undergoing a sixty million dollar loss, all through following years of 2005, 2006, and 2007."

"So who would pay seven hundred thousand dollars for stock in a company showing such a loss?" asked the CO.

"That is the 'everyone lived happily ever after' ending to the Clinton fairy tale," Kurt continued, laughing.

"It seems, according to the same public records filed at the same time, that Accoona listed, as one of its major owners, and also named as an official partner of this Accoona Corporation, none other than the China Daily Information Corp, a subsidiary of *China Daily*. This is a wholly owned corporation, operated and run by the Red Chinese government. It was also described as its official English language newspaper."

"Eureka," the CO exclaimed. "It was Chairman Hu then who

paid the seven hundred thousand dollars for the worthless stock. So the Clintons are still very much on the leash, still beholden to Hu," adding, "but why did the foundation not disclose that the purchaser was Red China?"

"Under American law," Kurt commented, "charities are not required to disclose the identities of their donors or the buyers of any stock holdings. Actually, by Clinton's failure to disclose that information, it double discloses that our Chairman Hu is the culprit."

"Chairman Hu must have available to him some money hungry, top notch, American lawyers to be able to figure that out."

"Clinton's lawyers had already figured it out before Clinton even gave the speech back in 2004," Kurt intoned, chuckling. "I guess you could call all this legal maneuvering and the continuing Clinton cover up, 'The Clinton Legacy Code'."

A staff sergeant interrupted handing a sheaf of papers to the CO, which ended the Clinton discussion. The CO looked over the documents in his hand, commenting, "Looks like your 6-1-2010 to 6-20-2010 leave has been approved. That is, if I can also arrange someone to sub for you, which I surely can," adding, "My approval is hereby granted," as he signed Kurt's furlough papers. He handed them to Kurt, and then suddenly stood and saluted him, even though he was a junior officer, saying, "Burn their ears off."

June 8, 2010 was a clear, beautiful Colorado day. The mountains loomed large and foreboding in the background, as Kurt and Mary watched the twin engine Cessna come in on its final approach, and make a beautiful three-point landing at the short and narrow Colorado Springs airstrip.

As Blitz taxied up to the waiting passenger, Kurt gave Mary a long, lingering kiss, saying, "I'll be back on the fifteenth or sixteenth. Thanks for bringing me to the airport."

Mary tried to remain cool, calm, and collected, but the knowledge that Kurt was going into a potential Washington DC wolf den, was unnerving to her. She was fully aware of what unrestrained government power encased in the wrong hands can do. She, however, mustered all her placid outward appearance, and smilingly told Kurt, as he stepped onto the Cessna wing to get into the plane, "I love you so very much."

The flight east was without problems, and Kurt and Blitz arrived fresh in the early evening at the Richmond airport, where the Senator's staff efficiently whisked them to the familiar Watergate Hotel.

However, the next several expert testimony filled days were hectic as they appeared before the Oklahoma Senator's committee. Their expertise went as planned with both Kurt and Blitz providing sworn testimony concerning the beleaguered F-22. They contended that only two hundred three of the magnificent, best in the world, multi-role, combat aircraft had been produced, as of June 10, 2010, and actually been built, or contracted for. This was true even though the Air Force had earlier authorized the building of one hundred fifty more. That order was now in jeopardy due to its being reneged on by the present Democrat, liberal, pacifist, Congress.

Blitz then warned the Committee, "If sufficient new F-22's are not manufactured, our American manufacturer will have to close down its production lines."

Kurt added, "Obama Administration strategists can't seem to get beyond their mindset of assuming all wars are of the guerilla Mid-East type warfare. It clearly dominates our military's thinking. The F-22 successfully combines several key technologies in this single fighter aircraft. The resulting plane is so stealthy that its enemies can only aim any return fire on some birds that may happen to be flying by."

Blitz testified, "The F-22 is the only US combat plane in the world which can avoid modern air-to-air missiles. It can also penetrate, unscathed, at mach plus speeds, deep into enemy territory, and it does not need afterburners."

This contention was countered by allegations the F-22's growing cost which have admittedly risen above its early estimates made three years ago. It is now an outrageous Three hundred thirty-nine million dollars per aircraft. Kurt agreed that this should be looked into, but told his crossexaminers, "The Congress, by changing the number originally approved from seven hundred sixty-two to six hundred forty-eight to four hundred forty-two to three hundred thirty-nine to two hundred seventy-seven, and now to only the one hundred thirty-four built, must remember that the original technology development costs still remain the same. Each time the Congress lowers the numbers ordered, it automatically increases the per unit cost. It would be much more efficient to order as many as possible."Blitz concluded his day's F-22 testimony, saying, "The actual per unit cost, as originally estimated, would be only one hundred thirty-six million per aircraft. He also told the Committee the same ruse was also used by the liberal pacifists to downgrade the number of the outstanding B-2 Spirit Bombers to only twenty-one, which of course drove their individual costs into the stratosphere. The initial Air Force B-2 plan was to build thirty-two of them. This accounted for the liberal's criticism as to the excessive cost of America to obtain these outstanding types of aircraft. We need B-2's and F-22's in order to properly defend America."

Thus the testimony concluded for the day.

The following day, June 11, 2010, testimony before the Committee continued, this time dealing with the proposed Obama-Russian START II Treaty.

Blitz blistered the talks as unnecessary, pointing out that the present START I Treaty, signed by Bush II in 2002, actually confessed to the world, and to our enemies, the non-active role of all things nuclear in American military strategy. It also clearly showed to our enemies that the new American strategy to try to develop precision-guided conventional weapons for use in long range targets, which in practice, leaves nuclear development, and the dangerous nuclear tipped missiles only in our enemies' domain. It becomes more ominous as there is no way the US can determine who, or which enemy may, or may not be testing nuclear weapons underground.

Blitz further testified, "America is, in effect, unilaterally disarming," adding, "If we were to abide by the strict concepts of START II, it would also severely impede, if not halt, our so-called, long range, precision-guided conventional weapons' system strategy, which we are presently embarked on."

Blitz concluded, saying, "If an enemy, such as China, then, in addition, embraces space based warfare weapons using lethal nuclear missiles, it would put the US public in great danger, with little likelihood of counter-action."

Kurt's turn at testifying, came with his cross-examination by one of the Committee's liberals asking, "Are you aware of the fact that both Japan and Australia, which, as part of the International Commission on Non-Proliferation and Disarmament have lauded the Obama

Administration for providing world leadership in an effort to promote cuts in nuclear arsenals, and also to provide sustenance to renewing worldwide non-proliferation treaties?"

"I read the media reports on this matter," Kurt admitted. "It is also reported that Vice-President Biden, National Security Advisor General James Jones, and Senator Kerry, Chairman of the Foreign Relations Committee, have already discussed these possibilities with the Commission, and the Australian delegate is quoted as saying, 'I got a very, very positive impression of serious commitment from President Obama to really do some game changing in this area.' If this quote is accurate, it renders the American people in great jeopardy."

That testimony caused the Chairman to bang his gavel, saying, "Such opinions are out of order," adding, "The Committee will stand in recess while this matter is reviewed."

Taking advantage of the recess, the Oklahoma Senator, Blitz, and Kurt tried to discuss what further matters they wanted to get out to the public, if they could.

Kurt suggested some mention could be made of EMP or the Electro-magnetic Pulse possibilities, and that it was becoming more and more a reality with Obama's disarmament and anti-cyberspace posture, and that the US should be very concerned about it. They mutually agreed to try to open up the subject for Committee discussion.

As the gavel again fell, re-opening the Committee session, it was obvious the Democrat Chairman was highly annoyed, saying, "From this point, it will be out of order to go into testimony of how a specific weapon system would, or would not, affect the US citizenry. I am ruling that it is beyond the scope of this hearing."

Following the Chairman's outburst, the Oklahoma Senator, changing the subject, asked Kurt, "Tell me about this phenomenon called EMP and America's ability to defend against this electro-magnetic pulse possibility."

As Kurt began his answer to the question, the Democrat Chairman inadvertently threw his gavel, which bounced harmlessly on the floor, saying, "This Committee hearing is ended. This Committee is now adjourned."

Obviously shaken by Kurt's expertise, his face showing bright red, lectured Kurt, complaining, "I'm extremely angry with you, Mr. Reitz, you insist on saying and doing things I specifically ordered you not to," as he had an attendant pick up the discarded gavel. "You are very close to being in contempt of this Committee," pointing his finger toward Kurt.

Kurt responded, smiling, "I thought I was responding to this Committee's responsibilities," adding, "It was Buddha who, in responding to a similar problem said, 'Holding on to anger is like having a hot coal in your hand, and then throwing it at someone you are mad at. It is the thrower who is the one who gets burned.'"

The Chairman, livid, rose up, and lunged forward at his desk, as several liberal Senators moved to restrain him, while at the same time, the Oklahoma Senator's Aide moved to conduct Kurt outside the Hearing Room.

The media, however, had already recorded the exchange for posterity, and the public.

CHAPTER XIX
EMP EXPOSED

The following day, both the New York and Washington, DC, newspapers featured, but placed inside the front pages detailing the altercation, which had occurred between Kurt and the Democrat Committee Chairman.

Various reporters who printed it across the nation, also did it in a way that downplayed the matter. The Committee Chairman was given twice as much space than Kurt, to refute his so-called "outburst", as being mostly political rhetoric, and much ado about nothing.

The next few days Kurt, shunned, became well aware that all of Washington was intentionally sidestepping him, as if he was a carrier of the bubonic plague.

Blitz, as a joke, kept poking him in the ribs, in his kidding "don't let it worry you" fashion, but both were astounded at the continuing media, and political control that the Washington power brokers had, over what Kurt and Blitz had considered to be vital public information.

The next to last day of Kurt's furlough, June 18, 2010, however, unexpectedly, a request came in from C-Span, asking, since they had had a cancellation, if Kurt could appear on a half hour call-in program.

"See, I told you not to worry," Blitz chided. "Things somehow work out when you are right," adding, "Let's get to work on this unique opportunity to inform the public."

C-Span opened its presentation, as its host began by asking, "Were you not aware the Committee Chairman had earlier established that testimony dealing with effects to the American citizenry was not in order at the Hearing?"

"I complied with his ruling," Kurt responded. "I did not go into that aspect at the time I testified. I only intended to show that electro-magnetic pulse was a phenomenon that must be considered a part of America's missile defense, which testimony was in order."

Kurt quickly used the opening to then contend, "I intend to go into EMP more fully on this program. I am actively inviting all Americans to call in and ask any questions they may have as to the serious consequences of EMP."

"What is this EMP?" the host asked.

"Assume an enemy of the US wants to find a way to completely disable a big part of the American homeland, and also wants to do it in a way that would avoid the ready defenses that the US already have in place," Kurt related. "A surprisingly easy way proves this could be done, and is also almost impossible to detect, or to truly assess blame," adding, "All our supposed enemy has to do is launch a nuclear armed missile, either from his country of origin, or from his preconditioned ship floating somewhere off the coast of America, and let the missile rise up to five hundred miles. Then to place it over Chicago, or some other big US city, and by remote control, causing it to explode."

"How could that be a danger at five hundred miles up?" asked the host.

"The effect is unbelievably devastating," Kurt acknowledged. "It is, however, a matter of common knowledge among scientific groups. For some reason, its effects are not generally known to the American citizen. This type of nuclear explosion creates what scientists call the 'Compton Effect', which is the widespread scattering of gamma rays emanating in a series of separate pulses," adding, "Its effect will be to disable all US military and civilian electronics in the area covered, including hundreds of commercial transformers which distribute electric power throughout the nation."

"I don't understand," the host insisted.

"For instance," Kurt replied, "this program, and all TV transmissions would just go off the air. All of our refrigerators, lights, and radios would suddenly cease. We, instantly, would have no modern electronic communications between one another."

"If this is such a danger," asked the host, "why don't we, in the public sector, know about it?"

"That is a good question," Kurt responded. "That is what I am hoping to be able to do on this program."

"If an enemy did this to us," the host continued, "would we not then plant a nuclear bomb on them?"

"If we knew who, and where," answered Kurt, "and if we also had left, after any such attack, the necessary vehicles to do it, along with an available nuclear weapon. America, don't forget, has unilaterally disarmed itself, nuclear-wise, in the past few years."

"Assuming that what you say is true," the host responded, "how do you defend against EMP?"

"You will need a space-based missile system," Kurt responded. "Right now, and only since 2006, we have developed a limited land-based missile defense, with silos in Alaska and California, along with a ship launched missile system."

Kurt continued, "A space-based interceptor system would be the only practical defense against EMP. It would also have the capability to destroy an enemy nuclear missile as it is just getting off the ground, or just arising from a ship. It is at that point it would be easier to identify with our computers and moving slow enough, to give our defenses a better shot at it."

"Do we have the technical knowledge, and the scientists in the US, which are capable of creating such a space-based defense?" asked the host.

"The technology was already available during the Reagan Administration," Kurt replied. "It is called 'The Brilliant Pebbles Defense', and it was tested thoroughly back in the early 1990's, during the Clinton Administration, and found to work one hundred percent, but not developed."

"Why has this defense not been fully implemented," asked the host, "if EMP is such a danger?"

"That is also a good question," Kurt responded. "You should ask that question of the politicians, and the Pentagon defense planners and strategists, in the Bush I, Clinton, and Bush II Administrations," adding, "It is technically very do-able. It remains whether enough public opinion can be generated to overcome the overpowering disarmament pushers. They still seem to dominate these matters."

And so the telecast continued with a number of, now, newly interested Americans calling in. By the time the half hour telecast was over, Kurt had reached enough of the populace that a nucleus of opinion was forming to demand of the government some answers.

As the host was closing, he asked Kurt if he had some final words for his audience, and Kurt responded, "Our enemies must be put on notice that America will overcome all obstacles, and prepare the necessary missile defenses, including a space-based Brilliant Pebbles system. America will defend themselves in whatever way it needs to, if they are aware."

Kurt warned any possible enemies not to underestimate the will, or the power, of the American people. He closed, solemnly, with a quote from Ronald Reagan, who he noted, was the president who began the American missile defenses, "President Reagan told us, 'If we lose freedom here, there is no place to escape to. This is the last stand on earth.'"

Mary, waving, met the two engine Cessna as it landed in Colorado Springs with Blitz and Kurt on board. She carried two separate bunches of roses, taken from her garden, saying as Blitz tied down the plane to its overnight stop, "I was so very proud of both of you," she said as she handed each of them their bunch of flowers.

"Did you see the program on C-Span?" beamed Kurt.

"You were magnificent," Mary acknowledged. "I heard every word."

It proved to be a joyous, and yet serious, reunion for the three as they related what had occurred in Washington. Blitz congratulated Mary on her and Kurt's engagement, and gave her a bottle of vintage wine he had somehow found while they were in Washington.

Mary responded with awarding them with a bountiful meal, including all the trimmings. The finest gift of all.

The evening elapsed all too soon. Blitz and Kurt reluctantly retired to Kurt's apartment for the night, thankful of a good night's rest, following their several days of adventure in the nation's capital.

They both slept well in the knowledge that they, like Paul Revere, were spreading the message, America needs missile defenses.

The balance of the summer, and most of the fall of 2010 had gone by, when Kurt hurriedly contacted Blitz by cell phone on October 22nd. Kurt excitedly related, "I have obtained a transcript of some testimony of one of the Obama Assistant Secretaries of Defense. It looks like our EMP warnings are being followed up, at least in some official defense circles."

Blitz, who the Air Force had returned back to Seattle to conduct additional test flights on the F-XXII fighter, was conveniently, at a place in the Bowing Plant where he was able to talk freely, asked, "What, I repeat what, does it say?" laughing. "I didn't think it could happen."

"It confirms exactly what we told them about the effects of EMP," Kurt replied. "It warns of a large Chinese military buildup, which, they say, appears to be deliberate and a well thought out military strategy to invest in asymmetric warfare, cyber-warfare, and what they call a counter space capacity."

"Where did this testimony take place?" asked Blitz.

"It was at a hearing conducted on behalf of the House Armed Services Committee. It took place a few months ago," Kurt replied.

"That's funny," Blitz replied, "I was unaware of this hearing, and I usually know when and where they are going. I also usually know the agenda."

"The transcript," Kurt continued, "points out that the Chinese buildup is significant and that it includes what they call 'electric pulse weapons'. They concede that Chairman Hu is building this exotic electro-magnetic 'pulse' weapon, or EMP, and that they agree it can devastate electronic systems using bursts of energy."

Kurt continued, "Let me quote the undersecretary. He told the House Committee, 'The consequence of EMP weaponry is that you destroy the communications network. We are heavily dependent on sophisticated communications, satellite communications, in the conduct of our forces. We could be in a very bad place if the Chinese enhanced their capacity in this area.'"

"Looks like someone in power finally stumbled onto this well known information," Blitz remarked. "I hope it was somewhat as a result of our testimony, and the public participation C-Span presentation."

"I'm sure our bringing in the American citizen on this subject was a factor," Kurt surmised.

"The truth will out," Blitz responded. "We must do what we can to force the government into the development of a vigorous American space strategy, including using the Brilliant Pebbles technology," adding, "There is one good report sent to me. It is of a program underwritten by the Air Force. They have produced technology to enlarge US capabilities in the accessing on all enemy's computer information systems. Supposedly the equipment is able to listen in on their computers, completely undetected, and without tipping them off, it also is supposed to be able to filtrate any and all information inside these computers," adding, "The report contends this technology then is able to strip the enemy computers of all their information, by, as they say, 'Deceive, deny, degrade, and destroy.'"

"Maybe it will help our computer system here at the Mountain," Kurt exclaimed, "but the US still also needs a surefire way to be able to destroy any incoming enemy missiles, after we discover them."

"One thing at a time," Blitz replied, "is evidently the best we can do. Oh-oh. Sorry, have to hang up. Got a meeting in five minutes. Will call you in November," adding, "As somebody says, 'Clear supremacy is often the best and surest deterrent.'"

"I hope and pray our Pentagon strategists are coming around to believe that," Kurt told himself, as he faced an empty cell phone receiver.

CHAPTER XX
CHINA CONTROL

Mary had, unfortunately, agreed, several months earlier with her persistent, local, Colorado Springs School Board, to stay on through the school year 2011. This agreement was by special request made by many of the parents who wanted her to teach their children. This was also prior to her engagement to Kurt. This contract impediment was now a thorn in her side, as both she and Kurt now wanted to proceed to a wedding date.

Major Kurt, however, also had impediments of his own. His Air Force enlistment period was due to end in July of 2011, but due to the sensitive, critical nature of his job, his Cheyenne Mountain CO had invoked an usually unused provision of the law, which allowed the military services to extend tours of duty an additional six months.

As a result, and then by mutual agreement, Mary and Kurt set their final marriage date for December 23, 2011 at Kurt's Germantown Lutheran Church. This date was certain, and no one would, or could, dare to change it.

The unmarried condition of Kurt did, however, allow him more time to work on his fighter designs while alone in his apartment. The continuing problems with China, however, negated any sharing of these plans with Bowing engineers, as the technical outgoing between the company and Chairman Hu became more and more obvious.

Kurt's plans and specifications now filled three briefcases. Blitz did, however, reassure him, that specific details of the F-XXII he was testing, had not been surrendered to China. This was part of the agreement Blitz's test pilot command structure demanded, and individual trusted engineers at Bowing assured him the promise was being kept by the company.

In their monthly cell phone get-togethers, Blitz also told Kurt that, as part of his testing, he was able to practice extensively in experimenting with the new, constantly, updated air-to-air missiles Bowing engineers had nearly perfected. They still had some work to do on them, but Blitz was excited about their value, telling Kurt, "If they work correctly, and carry sufficient arms, they could very well eliminate Kurt's anxiety about seeing Chinese missiles and not being able to do something about it.

On April 11, 2011, following Easter services at their church, Mary and Kurt were eating dinner at Mary's apartment, lamenting the fate of several of Mary's kinfolks who, due to the continuing Obama-Democrat deficits, being pushed through, a more and more reluctant Congress, lost their longtime jobs, with some big, some small, long established American companies.

Kurt commented, "In one respect, you and I are lucky. Both of us have some level of government, which pays our salaries. Government seems to be the only entity which can guarantee their worker's pay, and I suspect they are only printing extra money on weekends to do it."

"That," Mary replied, "and their continued selling of our birth rights to Red China. Is there not something we can do about it before November 4, 2012?"

"Aroused American citizens," Kurt responded, "took away some of Obama's majority in the House, in November 2010, but even though forty-three Republicans now grace the Senate, still due to the usual continuing traitorous GOPers, who can be counted on to give Obama his filibuster proof Senate vote, we can't do away with the bigger problems."

Kurt continued, between long, tasty bites of Mary's dinner, "But the biggest problem for America, has been the pandering to China of Bush II, and the up anteing of the Obama's same pandering, and the deficit spending, financing it all with outsourced American money, which Chairman Hu has conveniently stashed away, and uses to buy US assets. Hu is a master at manipulating and maneuvering greedy money seeking Americans," adding, "Chairman Hu now has two trillion dollars in foreign exchange, most of it in dollars. He, wisely, continues to buy up our treasury bonds, even though he knows he will lose money on them."

Kurt continued, "Chairman Hu, earlier, was also the largest investor in Freddy Mac and Fannie Mae, and, as a result, knowingly lost a big bunch."

"Why does he do that?" asked Mary. "He does not have to."

"Because Hu knows that by doing so, he will have more and more leverage over what America does, or can do, both commercial-wise or military-wise. He is holding our fate in his hands. He is playing America like a doll on a string."

Kurt continued between mouthfuls, "Obama, and his appointed disarmament people, who now run the Pentagon, the State Department, and comprise the liberal majority on the critical House and Senate Armed Services Committees, have, again, fooled the American people, with the help of the media. They have, in effect, disarmed America, and laid us open, undefended, before our enemies."

"How have they done that?" asked Mary.

"They did it by manipulating the details of the Obama 2010 Budget," Kurt intoned. "As usual, the details were hidden between the lines, and what really happens has to be pried out."

"Pry them out for me," Mary insisted.

"The media blared out, at the time, that Defense spending had actually increased over the 2009 Budget, but what was perpetrated, was an old congressional trick of inserting magic words into their budget. This simple maneuver, which consists of establishing a procedure which moves the 2010 Defense costs out of the supplemental budget, which requires an actual outlay of cash, and putting it into the base budget, which then can remain unpaid. These base budget costs usually are kicked ahead, requiring the necessity of future budget supplemental, to actually fund them."

"So, eventually, they will be paid?" Mary commented.

"Not necessarily," Kurt responded. "Obama put his commitment for fifty thousand additional troops under a base budget, and it will probably be paid soon under supplemental, but other crucial need Defense items, such as the F-22, and all kinds of vital necessary, missile defenses, plus the cyberspace Brilliant Pebbles satellite defenses will probably be kicked down the line, to a point, where it may not even be a factor anymore, and we may actually be unable to defend ourselves."

"The Congress won't let it got that far, will it?" Mary intoned.

"Congress, many times, can't look beyond its nose, or a better description would be its donor accounts," adding, "The airplanes our Air Force are now flying are so outdated that if they are not replaced by 2020, according to the General Accounting Office, eleven out of eighteen current US alert sites would be without aircraft."

"Why don't the American people respond?" asked Mary.

It takes repetition of these problems several times," Kurt replied, "to get some of them to respond. The strategic disaster of failing to fund our missile defense and that lack of foresight will put their children and grandchildren in great jeopardy. That is one way to make sure they finally know. When they understand that then things will finally move. But it will require some additional TNT under the media to provide that public information," adding, "Several months ago, former Admiral, and now Obama's National Intelligence Director, Dennis C. Blair, called the worldwide financial crisis, 'Our greatest threat,' but that fact does not seem to have registered with either the media, or the public, as to its effect on defense," adding, "But there is a bigger worry. Obama's Secretary of Commerce happens to be a Chinese-American by the name of Gary Locke. As Commerce Secretary, Locke not only controls the census, and says he is going to use ACORN as his census counters, he also has a direct line to Chairman Hu. Locke is the former Democrat governor of Washington state, and his election happened at the same time Clinton was chosen president in 1992. Both of them were traitorously close to Chairman Hu's Chinese born money runner, John Huang, who also worked for the Commerce Department. If you remember, it was he who carried a suitcase full of money into the White House, and delivered it to Hilary Clinton. He also provided Locke, through Hu, ample campaign money for his successful governor's campaign."

"So, does that affect America now?" asked Mary.

"Obama, and his Commerce Secretary, after Obama was elected, intentionally issued a specific waiver to relieve China, of the longstanding 1999 export control law, which provided some reasonable control over our continued transfer of American high technology assets," adding, "A former congressional investigator, who looked into it, said that Locke remains totally under the control of Triad gangsters and Chinese military agents. He also confirms through the Pentagon's last annual report, that China continues its systematic effort to obtain dual use and military technologies through legal and illegal means. China has not let up on its aggressive and wide ranging espionage, stealing anything which is technical in America."

"Hasn't that let up, changed since the recessionary downturn of the economy?" asked Mary.

"Several months ago," Kurt responded, "a Chinese native, by the name of Li Fengzhi, who was an integral part of Chairman Hu's Ministry of State, Security Intelligence Service, defected to America. He applied, at the time, for political asylum, and still has not had it granted, which indicates the continuing power Chairman Hu has over the Obama Administration, and his disarmament advisors," adding, "Mr. Li says he was employed by the ultra China group known as MSS, which is basically a control police, patterned after the old Soviet KGB. Its job is to maintain communist control for Chairman Hu."

Kurt continued, "Li says he was deeply involved in continuing Chinese domestic repression, and in the ultimate arrests and imprisonment of the Chinese underground Christian churches. It is a critical matter for China to keep control of the people, and doing so makes for widespread suffering and hardship," adding, "But Li also acknowledges that all of China's spy agencies are continuing to send spies to infiltrate the US intelligence services wherever it can. China spends tremendous amounts of resources to collect information. Li also related much time and effort is also spent to try to sensor the internet. It is important for Hu to prevent the Chinese population from knowing what is going on outside of China."

Kurt continued, "Li told us he was born in Northern China in 1968, began his agency work in the Provincial Intelligence System, and then was promoted into MSS. He, like other agents, then was sent to America to obtain a doctorate, and to familiarize himself with America, and an American university. He maintains that there are thousands of trained communist Chinese intelligence agents focused on the US, posing as diplomats, journalists, business representatives, and academics. They also make full use of living in America, Chinese immigrants, legal or illegal, by intimidating them into functioning as semi-professional information gatherers."

"There must be some way to blunt this continuing Red China's insistence on starting a war, and trying to destroy America?" Mary responded.

"There may be a way," Kurt ventured. "It appears kind of like a rainbow forming. Its usual array of colors, gathering. It is now more clearly coming together. While our Chinese rainbow is, at present only an imaginary mist, it is beginning to fill out, and is getting stronger."

Kurt continued, "Mr. Li gives us a solid clue of this possibility. He obviously has accepted some form of Christianity, which he attributes to ruing his anti-Christian work in China, and also being close to our Christian concepts while in college in America," adding, "Consider that in 1960, there were only a few million Christians in China. Today, even conservative estimates put the number at three hundred million, which is almost a third of China's population. Also consider that most of these new, searching Christians are foes of Chairman Hu, and they exist in underground churches. Hu and his storm troopers, plus his party hierarchy, spend all of their formal and informal National Peoples Congresses consisting of twenty-five hundred hardcore communist leaders, talking mostly about how to keep the people quiet, and how to beef up their mainland China intelligence agencies in an effort to identify, and to arrest, Christians, and then to kill them, or incarcerate them in work camps. The Peoples Congress recently gave their local communist police chiefs situated in all of China's widespread three thousand counties, specific anti-people training in handling local protests and disorders."

"Will this really affect us?" asked Mary.

"Chairman Hu is obviously worried," Kurt explained. "They don't want any sudden uprisings, or surprises. Their anxiety is also heightened by the ongoing economic turndown. This has further led to misery, to layoffs, to closing of plants, and to further disrupting of China's rural areas," adding, "When you have at least eighty percent of the people already against you, and then, at least, one-third of those already in an organized, hard to ferret out, underground Christian church, his anxiety can be clearly understood.

Chairman Hu could suddenly have real big, bad, troubles, plus, he really does not know if he can trust his police, or security. Look at Mr. Li. He had a good deal under Chairman Hu, but chose to defect."

Kurt took a final bite of the delicious eatery in front of him, and then commented, "Look Mary, all this is conjecture. I don't know if it will happen. I also don't know how effective Chinese Christians would be at revolting. I do know some of Hu's police forces have mutinied, and joined with the people in riots in rural areas. I do know that nations can be changed when you have a country as big as China, loaded with one point three billion diverse people and races. I do know that the Christian concepts relating that God and Christ, love and know about, care about, and want to help each individual Chinaman, must be overpowering to a people who have spent centuries as only so much fodder and beanstalks. God's personal, real love, gives them and their families a heart rendering stake in the world, and in Heaven. It could bolt and bust Chairman Hu's communist China, like a stroke of lightening," adding, "add to that some Christians conclaves on China's borders also do all they can to help China's underground Christians."

"That's something I did not know about," Mary intoned.

Kurt, laughing, told her, "In the Himalayan foothills of Northern Burma, now known as Myanmar, is a large group of Christian Burmese tribesmen, who over the years, associated with the main tribe known as the Kachins. They all live along Red China's southwestern province of Munnan, and have, for thirty years, fought several guerilla wars with Chairman Hu's troops, beating them to a standstill. They have now evolved into the Kachin Independence Army, which is a good, strong, modern, well armed, military force. This army sits on China's border, and can be counted on to give Hu continuing troubles."

"Maybe our trust should be in God," Mary offered, "rather than in a government, a Congress, and a Pentagon, which time after time fails to defend us," adding, "Do you think our present Obama Administration will somehow see the light?"

"Back in Germantown, Iowa, we have a saying," Kurt intoned. "It claims appropriately, 'You deal with the same dogs, you end up with the same fleas.'"

CHAPTER XXI
GO TELL IT ON THE MOUNTAIN

July 11, 2011, the day of the end of Kurt's official Air Force obligation, came, and then went, as his Cheyenne Mountain commanding officer exercised his legal option to retain Kurt for an additional four to six months for security reasons.

"I have two System Review Expert Trainees, training at Peterson AFB, in Colorado Springs, but they are not ready yet," the CO acknowledged. "Until they are fully declared experts, I will not use them."

"Why don't you send them for training to the Mountain?" Kurt intoned. "I will help you train them."

"Would you do that?" the CO replied. "I will try to get their transfers made in the next few days. That would greatly relieve my mind if I know you are on the job."

July 12th, however, was a day off, and Kurt called Mary to arrange a nice afternoon ride in the nearby Colorado mountains. He also decided to try to make his July monthly call to Colonel Blitz, who, he discovered, was presently working out of an Air Force base in Texas.

When Blitz answered, he began the conversation by saying, "I'm so mad, I could spit, whatever is the most toxic liquid I can find, directly at our liberal disarmament army, some of whom now occupy, and run, an important defense agency, known as the NRO or the National Reconnaissance Office."

"Is that the agency that is supposedly in charge of buying, building, and operating a satellite system?" asked Kurt.

"That is the one," Blitz replied. "However, they are not buying, building, or operating anything. Several months ago, they were fighting the Air Force, bitterly, to take control of the recon office. They won that battle, unfortunately. However, since taking over, the whole thing has bogged down."

"What do you mean?" asked Kurt.

The Air Force people, who first ran it, originally contracted to buy and operate two commercial imagery satellites. They wanted to use our current technology to create a sophisticated satellite spying apparatus. They dubbed it 'Broad Area Surveillance Capability' or BASIC. Each satellite set up was to cost approximately three billion dollars, but it would allow still images, as it circulated the earth twice each day, which then could be pieced together showing clear surveillance of enemy troop movements, spot construction of suspected missile and nuclear sites, and any new military training, or operating facilities."

"Wow," Kurt intoned. "If a single satellite can pass over one spot twice a day, it would make it tough for Chairman Hu to try to hide things."

"The problem is," Blitz responded, "since the disarmament people took over, those satellites, which actually should be operating, are not operating. The contracts might have been let, but I don't see any satellites. Obviously, the people running it are catering to the Obama policymakers in Washington."

"Same old story," Kurt offered. "The Obama Administration, just like it was in the Bush Administration, they do not want to offend Chairman Hu."

"The Pentagon director of what remains of a satellite control Air Force office has bitterly complained, saying, 'The military has to submit their satellite requests to the Office and then the civilians prioritize our missions.' It's a hell-of-a way to run an army," Blitz concluded. No working satellites. No intelligence. Very little Army."

"The Obama people are equally very busy in their efforts to limit, in numbers, even more than under Bush, the actual US deployed strategic nuclear warheads, in their ongoing discussions with the Russians," Kurt commented. "Predictably Republican Senator Lugar has also joined Obama, in pushing this big disarmament bid with Russia, which should also make Chairman Hu, not only happy, but ecstatic," adding, "They stumble over one another to see who can strip America of its defenses, the fastest, with the mostest.

"Since Obama has been in charge of our armed forces, and of our strategic defense," Kurt complained, "you have a right to spit, and spit often. He has, when you look at it closely, cut military and defense funds by more than fifteen percent, which will not allow us to fight in cyberspace, or anywhere else. In fact, the biggest part of the military budget goes to personnel costs, such as health, recruitment, and to pay for the continuing Mid East conflicts in Iraq and Afghanistan. There is not even enough in the present budget to replenish the states' National Guard with new or repaired equipment to replace what was destroyed by being used in Iraq," adding, "Obama's insistence on denuclearizing America will also extend the time necessary to assure America of the viability of our neglected nuclear stores. There has not been the necessary underground testing of our nuclear arsenal in several years. That is directly tied to the underfunding, and continued congressional refusals to allow the same. The biggest destroyer of our military, however, is if Obama finally wins in his continuing attempts to repeal the present law, which prohibits homosexuals from serving in the military. If the Congress permits such a horrendous thing, you will see the military really fall apart. There is no other single factor which will cause more conflict to most soldiers than being forced to live with a known homosexual."

"You hit it right on the head," Blitz agreed, "but what also really shakes me up, is Obama's use of his fancy words, and liberal congressional fancy footwork, to cover up their false facts. Obama, and his liberals in Congress, plus those in his Administration, are lying through their teeth to the American people about the true status of the state of our American nation, and of our diminishing ability to be able to defend against this ever growing list of enemies, and their weapons. A nuclear war – both in cyberspace, and on the ground, is a definite, real, probability. The American public is at great risk, and they are not being told of this catastrophic disaster that could befall their children and grandchildren," adding, "China is not inviting us to a tea party when it engages two hundred fifty thousand engineers and technicians in their hurried scramble to create cyberspace weapons. China has launched twenty to twenty-five new military satellites in just the last several months. Each satellite they put into space has as its main purpose, US military surveillance. Chairman Hu is obviously zeroing in on America, and the American people don't have a clue of the danger they might be facing."

"So what are we going to do? What can we do about it?" Kurt muttered. "We keep yelling to everyone, of the overwhelming dangers. However, it seems to float away in the thin Colorado air. People must think I'm nuts."

Kurt continued, "Enough of my wailing. Tell me what you are doing down in Texas?"

"The Air Force sent me down here to test out a sample of one of their modified, F-35's," Blitz responded. "I can tell you, without qualification, if the liberals think this plane will replace the F-15 and the F-16 as our main fighter plane in the next ten years, they are, in turn, crazy, or stupid, or both," adding, "There is good news, however, the Bowing engineers are already demanding that my CO send me back there to test their newest modifications to our unbeatable F-XXII, along with their modifications to the air-to-air missiles they also want tested. I'm slated to return to Seattle on September 1, 2011."

"I hope you and Bowing can get Obama, and his liberal Congress, to quickly approve of the F-XXII," Kurt commented, then noting the fleeting time, said, "I got to go. I got a date with Mary this afternoon."

"By all means, go," Blitz laughed. "I'll call you in September from Bowing. I wish I had such good duty."

Kurt hurried to turn his computers over to his substitute Expert teammate, and then covered the few miles between the Mountain and Colorado Springs, in record time. He skipped lunch in order to arrive at Mary's at the appointed time of 2:00 p.m.

"I brought a basket of goodies," Mary said, placing the food in the back seat. "It will make a nice supper in the mountains."

"I hope I can raid that basket sooner," thought Kurt to himself, "I don't think I can make it 'til supper."

Their mountain drive took them up the ever winding roads to Pike's Peak, and an opportunity to view the Pike Museum at the summit, along with several relaxing hours of mountain driving in displays of untold beauty all over the Colorado mountains, including some spectacular views of the lowlands from time to time.

An hour into the trip, Kurt was rewarded with an extra chicken breast from Mary's basket, after claiming sudden hunger.

The sun, however, was ever moving at its fast pace toward the west. It had wandered into some ominous looking black clouds, when they mutually decided to make use of a roadside table offering a view, allowing them to have their splendid picnic supper amid such spectacular mountain surroundings, plus, all to themselves."

"The rain looks like it is going to stay west of us," Kurt commented, as he sunk his teeth into more chicken, and Mary's potato salad.

They continued their small talk with some colorful view interruptions as they commented on one sight or another. This lasted through most of their supper, when Kurt, unthinking asked, "How are your kinfolks doing? Those that lost their jobs?"

"A few have taken advantage of local community technical schools and qualified as various medical technicians," Mary replied, rubbing her eyes. "That job field is still open, and the pay is not too bad," adding, "but a few are still collecting unemployment. Is there any hope this recession will be over anytime soon?"

"The problem is," Kurt responded, "the money power people, mostly in the US, don't want a solution that does not give them complete access to the taxpayer funds that make their financial situation equal to what it was before they put into motion the very things that caused this continuing recession."

"What do you mean?" Mary asked.

"These power brokers conceived of the destructive money making schemes called derivatives. These plans are usually gambling criminal acts. It made them an income of billions of dollars. To do it, however, required several legal changes to be enacted for the benefit of the big derivative banks, which they then used to pull off their criminal schemes. The Congress, as usual, duly complied, along with the equally culpable Clinton and Bush, who for some campaign donations, or a fee, they intentionally changed the laws which made banks, banks. It, in effect, made those banks into little more than gambling casinos. After a few years, reaping greedy, big profits, derivatives started to fall apart. Essentially, what happened is the derivative holding gambling casinos did not have the cash necessary to pay off the unforeseen probability; what would happen if the gamblers won. Thus, the curtains came down on their money making schemes. The taxpayer, who Congress then involuntarily recruited to put on the line to pay for their mistakes, became the fall guys. The taxpayer not only has to bail out those greedy big derivative American banks, but also bail out several derivative banks located in Europe," adding, "It makes me truly sick. Not only are Obama and the Congress sticking the taxpayer to make whole these culprits who caused the recession problem, but the facts underlying are protected by the media. Even after all these months, the media still has not leveled with the American taxpayer regarding how these problems came about. Not only did their derivatives destroy the taxpayer's bank accounts, and their retirement accounts, but also reduced the value of all American's assets by at least a third."

Mary, listening attentively, seemed puzzled, asked, "Why? Why has this kind of thing ever happened before? If so, I never was aware things could get this far out of line."

The evening shadows were quickly lengthening as happens so stealthily in the mountains. Kurt, with big bites, finished off the last of his picnic supper, and explained as he saw it, "The collapse of the USSR's empire back in the 1990's, was similar. Criminal communist operators in Russia, who were completely acquainted with the Russian production system, along with their criminal minded associates abroad, both in America and in Europe, managed to succeed the communist in the downfall. They created basically a criminal based government in Russia. They gleefully, and unhindered, plundered over two hundred fifty billion dollars in actual cash from various former Russian Treasury sources. Then after the complete Soviet collapse, they vacated their way out of Russia, carrying several suitcases filled to the brim with cash, including mostly one hundred dollar bills. Purchases of prime real estate followed in London, Paris, Rome, and all along the fancy streets in Europe, and in the US. It was all paid for in cash," adding, "Along the same line, today, some foreign banks find Obama paying for their derivatives. One is the UBS Bank in Switzerland. This is the same bank that refused, and refuses, to divulge to American tax authorities, which wealthy US citizens have created major secret bank accounts, amounting to a couple of trillion dollars. There is no question in my mind that, if disclosed, they would reveal not only the old Russian-American accounts, but also the accounts of some of those involved in our present 'Derivative' setup."

Kurt looking at Mary's increasingly sad face, and at the same time, realizing the growing darkness, told her, "I really wish I had not brought up these subjects, especially, at the end of such a beautiful, and relaxing, day. We better pack up and get on the road, before it gets too dark," adding, "I want to make sure you get home safely."

Mary smiled, and then commented, as she held Kurt's arm, "You told me a great deal about those who sacredly promise to be my protector, such liars as Obama, and those liberals running Congress," adding, "It reminds me of a quotation from Plato, which is inscribed on one of the pages in one of my English books. I hadn't earlier thought much about it, but it does seem appropriate to describe the pickle America finds itself in today. The quote says: 'This, and no other, is the root from which a tyrant springs, he first appears as a protector,'" laughing, "Present company excepted, of course."

CHAPTER XXII
MOUNTAIN HOOK-UPS

Through the balance of July, 2011, Kurt, anxious to retire peacefully from the Air Force, marry Mary, and to resume the life he most wanted, as an Aeronautical Engineer, did all he could to hurry the qualification of the Systems Review Expert trainee that now had been assigned for training to him. His trainee was making good progress, but still was not yet fully ready.

Kurt, in anticipation of his retirement, had sent his credentials, and his resumes, to several companies. He had also received back some very attractive offers. He and Mary had spent many an evening checking out the credentials of those companies.

On August 2nd, he received his monthly call from Blitz, who excitedly told Kurt, "I just got a message from one of the head engineers at Bowing. They ran into problems with the air-to-air system, and the engineer remembered an old plan that we had given him months ago, which he thought might work to solve the problem. He wants you to come to Seattle, when I come on September 1st, and advise them about the problem."

"Wow," Kurt exclaimed. "That would be fantastic. I've got some furlough problems here, but, let me see if I can work it out," adding, "I'll cell phone you back this afternoon."

Hanging up, Kurt immediately asked his team mate Expert, computing alongside him, to keep an eye on Kurt's trainee, while he made ready to see the Cheyenne Mountain Commanding Officer.

With over three weeks of unused furlough still owing him by the Air Force, Kurt intended to insist that the CO grant him at least a week at the Bowing plant in Seattle.

"Your trainee is doing very well," chuckled his CO. "I am also very appreciative of your help in training him. I would judge by the last week of August, he could be ready. This would give you a few days to get ready for Seattle, and at least fourteen days there with the Bowing engineers."

Kurt, greatly relieved, notified Blitz he would be there with bells on, on September 1, 2011, and to get him a regal room at the local BOQ.

By August 29th, Kurt's trainee was all but certified, and his partner Expert promised to look after him. Kurt had also put together some thoughts, plans, and ideas, regarding the continuing air-to-air missile problems, plus a few others of his own thoughts.

Kurt easily made arrangements to fly on August 31st with an Air Force transport plane, which regularly made flights to Seattle. Everything was in readiness to leave.

On August 30th, a day he promised to devote to Mary, they met for lunch at a high quality, Colorado Springs restaurant, and both looked forward to a relaxing time.

"I've already sent my final retirement paperwork to my School Board," Mary commented, as they waited to be served by the waiter.

Kurt nodded, saying, "Looks like I can get my final discharge at least by November, so we will, I repeat, will be married on schedule, on the 23rd of December," adding, "Did you send the information he wanted to the officiating Germantown pastor?"

"Everything he wanted, and then some," Mary replied. "I really like that man. He makes doing these things so easy."

Mary then asked if Kurt had everything put together for his trip to Bowing.

Kurt responded, "Everything I need, except for you."

Mary smiled, and then asked, "A few days ago you mentioned that you had developed a computer breakthrough that you were also taking with you. What is that?"

Kurt paused while their waiter placed glasses of water on their table, along with a small bowl of soup for each, and then replied, "It's probably not of much interest to a civilian like you, but I think I have found a way to hook up to the information on my entire computer system at Cheyenne Mountain. That system can discover and observe missiles launched from anyplace in the world. I hope to direct it to the computer system in Blitz's F-XXII fighter plane that he is now testing, as an example."

"Is that so difficult?" Mary asked.

"Not after I thought of it," Kurt laughed, "and also tested it," adding, "For instance, it would, for the first time, allow a computer operator, riding side-saddle in Blitz's F-XXII, to have direct access to all the computer goodies that appear on the several banks of my extraordinary computers that I observe for several hours every day. It is the only true missile locater available in America. It would give those F-XXII flying defenders the chance to get a leg up on any nuclear missiles that might be fired by an enemy. Right now they don't have that capability."

"Have you told Blitz about this wonderful thing you put together?" Mary said looking at Kurt with obvious admiration.

"I have all the components stashed in several of my briefcases," Kurt replied, as the waiter again appeared bringing on their main course.

Kurt met his Air Force transport plane with Mary's help, on August 31st, and had an uneventful flight to Seattle. Blitz, unexpectedly, met him at the Air Drome, which the Air Force usually uses. He laughingly told Kurt that since he had reserved the regal BOQ room for him, right next to his humble hovel BOQ room, Kurt was therefore stuck with the costs of their semi-regal meal at the local Officer's Club mess.

They hurriedly chomped down their dinner, as Kurt told him about his computer hook-up ideas, and components. Blitz, amazed, wondered that such could be done, said, "The F-XXII is now sitting loose and will be all day tomorrow. It would be available to you if you want to try out those computer ideas," adding, "The Bowing engineer working on the air-to-air won't be here 'til September 2nd. He will then want to go over your ideas. Until then, you and the F-XXII are available to one another."

"It's nice to be available," Kurt chuckled.

September 1st proved to be a red letter day for Kurt. After enjoying a good night's sleep in his regal BOQ, which, as Blitz noted, meant

Kurt had a bureau with four drawers, rather than the usual three, and Kurt was allowed access to the F-XXII, all to himself.

Kurt marveled at the unique stealth air frame structure of the plane. He also recognized the incorporation of a few of his own stealth designs.

A computer, however, to Kurt, was still only another computer. He had no difficulty fathoming their distinction. After a few hours of fiddling with the dials, and installing some of his components, Kurt found that only a few of them needed any adjustments, or required any new or different circuits, but Kurt already had, in his briefcases, the necessary replacements. By 11:30 a.m., when Blitz showed up on the scene looking for a lunch mate, Kurt was already fully ready to try it. Prior to leaving Cheyenne Mountain, Kurt had alerted both his CO at the Mountain, and his longtime partner, Systems Review Expert, so they both would know that he was going to try to set up the F-XXII with the Mountain computer information, and Kurt knew they would be aware of any contact by him.

"Want to be in on the big test?" Kurt asked.

Blitz leaned easily into the cockpit, nodding, as he watched Kurt, sitting in the side-saddle, radio-computer-gunner-assistant pilot, part of the F-XXII canopy, move around a few knobs, make a few fine adjustments, and then state loud and clear, "Do you read me, Cheyenne Mountain?"

A few seconds later came a reply, "We read you."

"A-Okay," that was followed by, "I'm downloading some current information now."

Miraculously, the information contained in Kurt's Cheyenne Mountain bloc of computers, began registering on the F-XXII's computer screens.

"Hoo-ray. Hoo-ray. Wow," shouted Blitz, giving Kurt his best admiring whop on the shoulder, saying, "Nobody else in the world could have accomplished this feat."

Kurt attentively watched by Blitz, continued to access the information from the Cheyenne Mountain computers during several different attempts, each made more difficult in the next two hours, both skipping lunch, to make sure his computer hook-up would stay and remain constant, even if it was put under a constant cyberspace strain and sprain, and other possible re-doubts, but everything remained A-Okay.

At dinner that evening, Blitz told Kurt to keep the facts of his hook-ups secret for now, until Blitz could get an iron-clad agreement from the Bowing engineers to keep the set-up from being passed on to Chairman Hu.

The next morning, and extending well into the afternoon of September 2nd, Kurt, and Blitz, met with the Bowing engineer in charge of planning, building, and designing the particular air-to-air missile system.

Up to now, the system consisted of three separate sets of nine air-to-air missiles, engineered to be fitted in good order on Blitz's F-XXII. Blitz could conveniently fire the missiles by pushing only a single button, which also would release only one missile at a time.

Kurt and the Bowing engineer continued to be very busy the next several days, pouring over Kurt's ideas on transfiguring the missiles to gain different speeds and distances. These changes could be accomplished by redirecting their computer directions. It also required several, some simple and some complicated, adjustments to the F-XXII's computer system.

During this high tech time period, Blitz insisted on being ever present, either as a cheerleader for Kurt and the engineer, or in taking the F-XXII up for various aeronautical checks, usually with Kurt in the second seat, checking his new air-to-air computer adjustments. Blitz and Kurt, after each flight found that all their tests, tested out A-Okay.

Blitz told the Bowing engineer about Kurt's secret hook-up to Cheyenne Mountain from the beginning, and the engineer also agreed with Kurt and Blitz to keep that information confidential for now. He said he would need time to assure Kurt and Blitz that the information would remain confidential, then commenting, "It should be easy to do as at this point, only Blitz, Kurt, and I, and my designates, would have any access to the F-XXII."

Blitz had, over the several previous months of his flight testing the F-XXII, also made crucial adjustments to the original plane. His input allowed the plane to increase its fuel capacity by one-third, giving it the present ability to be able to reach the Asian continent, with only a fuel stop at Bowing's small, remote, unused, northern Hawaiian island, which contained a small fuel depot and a short landing strip, which Bowing used for special flights, plus a second fuel stop at Guam.

Blitz had also, during the same period, prodded the Bowing engineers to increase the explosive power of each air-to-air missile by three-fold, using the top smart bombs, and other, non-nuclear, armament located in the US inventory. Blitz had also fully flight-tested them, finding the improvements were A-Okay.

By the 9th of September, 2011, Kurt, Blitz, and the Bowing engineer had accomplished most of the air-to-air missile improvements they had set out to do.

The engineer profusely thanked Kurt for his crucial ideas, saying, "Without your input, we could never have accomplished these necessary improvements. I know you are getting out of the Air Force soon. I hope you will consider coming back to Bowing."

Kurt smiled, his chest swelled at the laudatory remarks, commenting, "I have several offers, and where I go will depend on my freedom to design, a strong assurance that my ideas will remain in America, and the full approval of my new wife."

"I hope to give you that complete assurance. Your plans and specs, if I have anything to do with it, will not go out of the safe in my office," the engineer promised. "What Bowing management does, sometimes imprudently, is as important to me, as it is to you."

Kurt smiled, and in an attempt to further avoid the subject, told the engineer, and Blitz, "I do have one more idea to present and try out on both you and Blitz, before I head back to Cheyenne Mountain."

Both looked at Kurt, their faces wrung with amazement, "You have another idea?"

Kurt laughed, and then pulled out a set of computer resets from one of his briefcases, saying, "It is of greater importance to be able to engage air-to-air with the most potent nuclear, or other equally lethal, missiles thrown at us by an enemy. It is also important that such a magnificent machine as the F-XXII would be able to change the missiles it carried to fit the target."

"What do you mean?" asked the engineer.

"He means, change the dynamics to allow a missile, if feasible, to be fired at an appropriate ground target, don't you Kurt?" Blitz intoned in a loud, but unbelieving voice. "Don't tell me you have found a computer way to do that?"

"I think I have," Kurt replied, exhibiting his set of computer resets to Blitz and the Bowing engineer. It should work. I would, however, need an hour alone with F-XXII's computer, and Blitz would then have to test it in flight."

"It's now 10:00 a.m. on September 10th," Blitz noted. I was going to take the plane for a test run it needs this afternoon. If you went with us, right now, to the F-XXII, would you be able to reset the computer to enter the new commands and circuits so I could finish my tests?"

"I should be able to easily," Kurt responded with confidence.

Kurt did reset the computer directions, although to change from air-to-air to air-to-ground, Blitz would have to push a locked slide button, which would extend from the main missile release button, but in the afternoon test of the F-XXII, everything worked well, with no problems.

The final thing Kurt did before leaving the F-XXII, for what he thought was the last time, was to send a computer message from the plane telling his fellow Systems Review Expert, located at the Mountain, he would be back in Colorado Springs on the 11th of September, and would then be back at his post at Cheyenne Mountain, at 8:00 a.m., Mountain time, on September 12, 2011.

That final evening of the 10th of September, 2011, Blitz and Kurt were treated to an extraordinary dinner, paid for by the Bowing engineer, who kept toasting both Kurt and Blitz throughout the same.

When a toast came up, sponsored by Kurt, to laud the entire Bowing Company, the engineer remained quiet.

Blitz also, shaking his head, refused, saying, "I've made some good friends among some long time cattle ranchers near where I'm stationed in Texas. They have a distinctive statement about what they think of the neo-Texans that are now making up a large part of Texas," adding, "They point out, 'Such are all hat, and no cattle.'"

"I suggest we toast to the fine Bowing engineers that built the F-XXII," Blitz concluded.

CHAPTER XXIII
SEPTEMBER 11, 2011

"*Good Lord! What time is it?*" Kurt asked himself, as he reached for his ringing cell-phone, and, at the same time, looked at his watch.

September 11, 2011, 0200 hours, his wrist watch recorded, as he answered his cell phone, saying, "Do you realize it is 2:00 a.m.?" Kurt almost shouted into the receiver.

"Sorry Kurt," was the reply. "This is extra important."

Kurt sat up in his bed as he recognized the voice of his longtime computer teammate, the Systems Review Expert who Kurt left in charge of his Cheyenne Mountain computers. "What is it?" he mumbled.

"They called me in to look at a strange missile launch," the Expert replied. "It looked like it originally came from a ship, somewhere in the South China Sea."

"What happened to it?" Kurt, now wide awake, responded. "Where is it now?"

"That's the problem," the Expert replied. "It looked like it was trying to get up to about five hundred miles in the stratosphere, when it suddenly failed at about three hundred fifty miles, and fell back into the sea. It must have been a dud."

"Five hundred miles," Kurt echoed. "That is the height of someone who would be attempting an electro-magnet pulse."

"That's what came to my mind," the Expert claimed. "That's why I called you. Thank God I had your cell phone number."

159

"It's got to be China," Kurt intoned. "No one else has the ability, or the maliciousness to do such a thing."

"I agree," came the reply, "especially since it was launched out of the China Sea area."

"Since China has taken the big war move, and it has declared war already, by its launching this missile, even though it was a dud," Kurt reasoned, "it is logical to assume that Chairman Hu will now launch other missiles," adding, "It probably will take them two or three hours to set up another launch ship to send up the next EMP missile. Who knows how many they might have in mind," adding, "We do know Chairman Hu has decided to try to fool us by launching them at sea, rather than from bases on Mainland China."

"What should we do?" the Expert asked.

"First, give all your computer details of the dud to the Mountain CO," Kurt replied. "Let him decide who to contact," adding, "I know of only one US missile defense capable of shooting down these EMP missiles in the time frame they are likely to be launched. That is our F-XXII test plane, and its updated missiles. It is now in its hangar here at Bowing. Keep me advised of any new launches based on five minute intervals, sent directly to the F-XXII's computer. I will awaken Blitz, and get the plane ready."

It seemed like it took an eternity for Blitz to answer his door after Kurt, now fully clothed in his uniform, rapped on his BOQ.

Finally, a sleepy-eyed Blitz peeked through a slightly opened door, muttering, "Its two thirty in the morning."

That changed quickly when Kurt told him his mission. Blitz did not doubt, or question, Kurt, and, even before he put on his uniform, Blitz called the night crew at the Bowing Hangar, and told them to fuel up to capacity, the F-XXII, and to attach all nine of its updated missiles.

"Going to try a night mission?" the crew chief joked, not knowing the true danger.

Blitz also called their associate Bowing Engineer, who, at first, would not believe Blitz, saying, "They wouldn't do such a thing, would they?"

By three thirty a.m., both Kurt and Blitz were at the hangar, talking with the crew chief, and checking over the installations of the updated missiles.

The crew chief kept a one-sided conversation going as to the mission, as neither Kurt nor Blitz discussed the missile situation.

The Bowing Engineer did, however, arrive at the hangar at 0400, just as Kurt was getting an update on the F-XXII computers from the Mountain, which told him that another missile had been launched, probably from a ship in the vicinity of the South China Sea. This missile had been put in orbit around the earth, and appeared to be moving to a generally higher, two hundred mile altitude with each orbit, and could be at the five hundred mile altitude after the second orbit.

Beaconing both Blitz and the engineer to the plane, Kurt told them, "Another missile has just been launched," and in a calm voice stated, "If my reasoning is correct, the missile could be in the electro-magnetic pulse position by 0700 Seattle time."

"So it is true," the engineer cried. "It is so dumb. So dumb."

"It is a fact," Blitz commented, adding, "Look, you should do two things. One, notify Washington, DC. Tell them what we know. Tell them also we don't know all the effects, but they should immediately try to disconnect all computers, and all electrical generators and grids, or other electric connections. It might help. The second thing," handing him Blitz's cell phone, "call your Bowing base in Hawaii. Tell them to be ready to fuel up the F-XXII in a couple of hours. I will be there."

Blitz, while the engineer complied, told the crew chief to wheel out the F-XXII, saying, "I want to get in the air as soon as possible. Is the fueling completed? Are the missiles attached?"

As the crew chief was nodding yes, and hurried to retrieve the airplane mobile mover, Kurt intoned, "What do you mean, 'I'. I'm going with you. This is the most critical America saving flight ever. You must have someone able to keep track of all the essential computer information from Cheyenne Mountain, and then to be able to calculate, and re-calculate, all the coordinates, and the cyberspace mathematics necessary, if you are going to have any reasonable chance at all to close down Chairman Hu's war. I assume that is what you will try to do."

"This could be a suicide mission," Blitz warned, nodding, "You have Mary. You have your wedding, and a million other reasons to live."

"If this can be stopped," Kurt replied, "Mary will be the most thankful that I was able to ride along," adding, "You also," laughing, "could not get me out of this cockpit with TNT. I'm going to call Mary and tell her, and warn her. I am going to do it right now."

It was 4:15 a.m. or, 0415 military, Seattle time, when the crew chief finally aimed the F-XXII straight down the main, darkened, runway, with Kurt already inside.

Kurt's cell phone call had wakened Mary from a deep slumber back in Colorado Springs. She started an uncontrolled crying when she began to fully understand the facts. Kurt told her he was going to go with Blitz on their hopeful adventure, flying blindly toward the West, but carrying the hope to stop this war from the Asian East. She wailed into the phone, "No. No. Don't go. I don't want you to go. You are only one of three hundred million Americans. Why do you have to go?" crying even louder.

Kurt sorrowfully hung up the phone with a final, "I love you."

At 4:30 a.m., Blitz and Kurt were airborne in the starless night, speeding toward Hawaii on their critical vital mission.

Kurt immediately monitored his F-XXII computer system keeping Blitz, fully informed of the progress of Chairman Hu's second missile. As they were approaching Hawaii, Colorado's Cheyenne Mountain computers kicked in again, and reported to Kurt, "It is now 0800 Colorado time, 0700 Seattle time. Unfortunately, it looks like the second missile has reached its five hundred mile stratosphere objective. It appears to be moving in an orbit past the American West Coast, and is nearing the East Coast. It is located somewhere between Washington, DC, and New York City."

After a pause, the Expert involuntarily yelled, "My God. The nuclear device aboard the second missile has evidently exploded," causing another pregnant pause, after which the Expert calmly stated, "I want to report that a third missile has been successfully launched from a third ship in the South China Sea. We will closely monitor its progress. It was launched at 0635 Seattle time. Estimated EMP time is 0900 Seattle time. We are putting together the coordinates of the exact location of all three launch ships, and will inform you of any new ship movements. We will also send you the information from the US East Coast as soon as we are able to obtain the same from a responsible authority."

Kurt dutifully started to report the bad news to Blitz, as he, at 7:30 a.m. Seattle time, was preparing to bring the F-XXII down on the short Hawaii landing strip, causing Blitz to say, "Save it 'til we get down. I need all my faculties to negotiate this landing."

While the Hawaii crew re-fueled the F-XXII, Kurt and Blitz had an opportunity to discuss their options. The crew at Hawaii knew that something was amiss, but did not know what. The chief complained that they had been warned by Seattle to "Stand by", and that something big had happened to New York City and Washington, DC, as all communications from there had ceased.

Blitz and Kurt continued conferring while the re-fueling was going on, and mutually agreed that the enemy missiles were being launched solely from these three ships, and all three ships were located in various places in the South China Sea. They also agreed that they might have been given a Devine break, since the first ship's missile was a dud, and nothing more has been reported of any new missiles from that ship, it may be out of action. They again determined that the time span from missile launch to EMP orbit was approximately three hours, however, the time span to re-set the two remaining missile launching ships to be able to launch more missiles, was still unknown at this time.

"I'll make that my first priority when we get back in the air," Kurt intoned. "I have the utmost confidence that between me, and the mathematical coordinates given me by the Mountain, I will be able to locate and identify all three ships, so that when we are within their range, we can take them out."

At 0745, the F-XXII was back in the air headed for Guam.

The Hawaii crew tried to get some information out of Blitz, but was unable, even though the crew chief made a cell phone call to Guam telling a crew there to expect the F-XXII to be there in a few hours, and to be ready to re-fuel it.

About two hours West of Hawaii, Cheyenne Mountain again came on the F-XXII computer, loud and clear. The expert related that the second missile was on its final orbit to reach a five hundred mile height, and probable EMP. Further that their computers indicated, at 0800

Seattle time, a second missile was being launched from the second ship. He would closely watch its progress, and report the same to Kurt. The Expert explained he could not rouse anyone he could trust from his usual New York, or Washington, DC contacts, and finally decided to call the air controllers at Cleveland's municipal airport, who did have some information. The Expert revealed, "Several commercial airliners operating over the East Coast area, at the time of the nuclear explosion, experienced total computer and electrical failure, and those not close to a proper landing area were lost. Cleveland confirmed there was absolutely no communication from Boston all the way to Roanoke, Virginia, and that that area had suffered total computer and electrical shutdown. Many deaths were occurring among the aged and the sick, because area hospital and nursing home generators had ceased to work. Cleveland said they also had reports of hundreds of auto and truck accidents occurring because the cities no longer had working traffic lights, or other traffic controls. It was labeled a mess," ending, "I'll be back when I can give you a better fix on this newly launched missile. Oh, oh. It looks like our orbiting missile is moving over the South Pacific Ocean, approaching somewhere near Los Angeles. Oh, oh. It has just exploded. I will try to find out where, and the damage."

Kurt told Blitz of the new developments, and also of the new EMP explosion taking place over the southern California, northern Mexico area.

"Too bad we are not within range," Blitz lamented. "Soon we will be able to try," adding, "We know now that each of the remaining two launching ships require at least four hours to re-set, before they can launch another missile. The second ship could be ready, as soon as 1000 hours or 1100 hours Seattle time. With a three hour orbit time, we should be able to have an opportunity to try to hit it while it is on its first orbit, and while its over a minimal damage area like the Atlantic Ocean.

An hour out of Guam, Cheyenne Mountain came on again to the F-XXII's computer. It brought the news that all of southern California, from Los Angeles down through the Mexican Peninsula, was completely without communications. The second missile, now proceeding from the second ship was also reported to be reaching its first orbit, and progressing steadily," adding, "We are also sending, herewith, our current coordinates as to all three ships. The first ship is obviously disabled, and is floating with the tide. The second and third launch ships have widened the gap between them, although they remain in the South China Sea area. The whole China Sea has very few ships. China probably is intentionally safeguarding its Navy."

The computer ended with the message they were trying to contact California, and would be back momentarily with new coordinates, along with up-to-date information on the just orbiting second missile from the second ship.

Within an hour, and prior to reaching Guam, about 1045 hours Seattle time, the computer suddenly set forth coordinates, and location numbers of the exact location of the new missile as it was continuing on its first orbit, all as requested by Kurt earlier.

"When it gets near the center of the Atlantic Ocean," Blitz intoned, "Have them send final estimated coordinates of its then location, allowing for a three minute, twenty second, add-on, and for them to stand by and report."

Kurt, understanding that they would try to shoot it down, busied himself with the necessary computer mathematics, and the crucial calculations which would achieve their goal.

"Center Atlantic Ocean reached," cackled the computer, "Final calculations with the add-on are...," and spit them out. Kurt eagerly made short work of each cipher.

Blitz yelled, "Are you ready Kurt?"

After an eighteen second pause, Kurt replied, "Ready. One. Two. Three. Go."

Blitz leaned forward and pushed the release button sending the F-XXII's first air-to-air missile on its way. Its speed put it out of sight quickly, but the missile made several obvious computer calculations on its own before it disappeared over the horizon.

Both Blitz and Kurt had their eyes fixed on their watches, as the computer belched, "Missile number two just exploded over the center of the Atlantic Ocean. The only thing discomfited are the fishes," adding, "Congratulations Supermen, Superman, could not have done it better."

CHAPTER XXIV
ZHON GNAMHAT

It was the boson mates who welcomed the F-XXII to Guam, but it was the top Navy brass who stood in line to see them off at 1130 hours, Seattle time. Fragmentary information about the EMP explosion over the East Coast, and the southern California West Coast EMP explosion, along with information about the absolute destruction of the next EMP missile, exploding harmlessly over the Atlantic, had finally reached Guam. The information came by way of Cheyenne Mountain, then to Bowing at Seattle, and then to the military command at Hawaii, who notified Guam.

Even a cursory look at the available information made clear that Blitz and Kurt were in command of what was the only current flying instrument, which could stop any additional EMP's. They were, indeed, heroes of the highest order.

Blitz, to protect his chariot, made sure he stayed with the F-XXII, while it remained on Guam.

"You never know when an Admiral might show rank and try to command the F-XXII, and then try to play hero themselves," Blitz told Kurt, who had just returned from a scouting trip to find some food.

"It would not be the first time," Kurt agreed, handing Blitz a sandwich and a cup of coffee.

Both Blitz and Kurt, in addition, went out of their way to not join the ever-growing clutch of Navy brass, as much as they could. Blitz urged the crew chief to move them out onto the runway early, just to avoid any mistake, or misunderstanding. The takeoff was smooth as the F-XXII again faced the east, heading west.

An enemy missile they knew, however, had been launched, and was fast approaching its first orbit. It was the most vulnerable at that point to the F-XXII's air-to-air missile, and Kurt immediately notified Cheyenne to give him the coordinates and other location data, as soon as possible.

"It looks like this missile will follow the path of the North Pacific, over the North Pole," then giving intricate mathematical data.

"Not too good this time," Kurt cautioned Blitz. "Orbit is to be over Japan, and then over the many North Pacific Islands."

"Ask them how close it will come to the North Pole," Blitz intoned.

The quick answer to Kurt's inquiry came, "Two hundred fifty miles north – south of the pole, and it will be there in eleven and a half minutes. On the Russian side of the pole," the computer added.

"Calculate the X mark at that point, plus four minutes, ten seconds," Blitz urged.

Kurt quickly made the critical, necessary, calculation, and had inculcated the same into the next to be used air-to-air missile, with in a ten minute span, and then told Cheyenne, "Stand by. Watch a point two hundred fifty miles north-south of the pole. Add in four minutes."

Kurt then announced, "Number two air-to-air loaded, cocked and ready to go. On the count of seven," which count he began as Blitz pushed aside the lock button, which loosed the air-to-air button to be activated at the seven count. The F-XXII's second air-to-air missile sprang to life, and moving from west to northeast, quickly disappeared over the horizon.

Kurt waited patiently, and confidently, for the explosion report from Cheyenne, watching his watch at the same time.

"Bingo," was the response, and the ever timely report from Cheyenne. "Right on the button. I hope the Russians won't be too mad. We are, you know, savaging their Siberian wolves."

Kurt involuntarily laughed aloud, causing Blitz to questioningly turn his head.

"Private joke," Kurt pled, "Siberian wolves are the biggest casualty of this successful Siberian caper."

Blitz smiled, and then admitted to Kurt, "Thank you for riding the F-XXII with me. I could not have accomplished any of our successes without you."

Kurt also cracked a smile at the admission, feeling the pride in his heart that came with their, so far, successful Far East adventure.

"Fuel gage full. Missiles at the ready," Blitz bragged. "We now can, even with bad odds, put a stop to Chairman Hu's Cyberspace War," adding, "What do you think? After we take care of the launching ships, where is the best place to try to land the F-XXII, Japan or South Korea?"

"Our fuel will get us within a few hundred miles of any of our intended targets. It should be enough to do that job, if everything else works the way it is supposed to," adding, "Our air-to-air missiles have worked to perfection so far. God is with us."

Blitz turned to Kurt, and nodded in agreement.

Kurt, then doing some additional calculations, told Blitz, "We have seven missiles left. Assuming we will need three to get rid of the launching ships, that will leave us with four."

"With only four," Blitz lamented, "and with a country which covers half of Asia, plus a billion people, how can four measly air-to-air missiles win a war?"

Before Kurt could answer, at 1230 hours, Seattle time, the computer blared out the news from Cheyenne Mountain, saying, "Ship Number Two has just launched missile number three. The coordinates, and location data of the three ships are as follows," detailing the same. "You will note the first ship has not moved, except for the tide. The second ship is now only a hundred miles from the ports near Beijing, and the third ship is moving south quickly, putting several hundred miles between them."

"Give me the coordinates, and the probable path of the newest launched missile," Kurt responded. "We will try to catch it on its way up," adding, "It helps that ship Number Two is relatively close by. That will give us a good chance at getting it while it is in its slow mode."

The computer information on the third EMP missile with an updated trail, followed, and Kurt hurriedly made his new calculations, revealing them to Blitz, after making the necessary adjustments on the F-XXII's third air-to-air missile.

In a matter of only seconds, Blitz loosed the plane's third missile, and watched it zoom to the west on its journey of hope.

The computer blared, "You got it just as it reached the height to send it into orbit, and when it was at its slowest," adding, "The explosion took place over the ice and snow of the Antarctic, but it was not at a height where it could create an electro-magnetic pulse. Congratulations from all of us to our heroes."

Both Blitz and Kurt smiled broadly, as Kurt responded, "We now have expended three missiles. Six left. Three for the three ships. Three left."

"If we forget about the dud ship, we would still have four," Blitz counted."

"But the dud ship might be put back on line," Kurt replied, "that could cause some real trouble that we would not be able to handle."

"You are right," Blitz admitted.

Kurt quickly made some additional calculations, and then told Blitz, "Ship Number One, with probable nuclear missiles remaining is drifting only a few hundred miles from the South China Sea's ports, where most of Chairman Hu's navy is situated. Likewise, ship Number Two, which fired the last missile is now extremely close to Beijing. We don't know if it still has nuclear missiles aboard, but probably does. Our first priority should be those two ships, and that priority will be coming up in a matter of minutes."

Blitz nodded, saying, "Calculate the necessary adjustments to air-to-air numbers four and five, and let's get them airborne. If we get lucky, we could set off Ship One, or Two's nuclear stores, which would raise havoc in Beijing, and the surrounding area."

"That will still give us four remaining missiles," Kurt commented, "plus one less for ship Number Three."

"Three is a lucky number," joked Blitz, "Lucky for us. Unlucky for Chairman Hu," adding, "Where do you think they should go?"

Kurt took a few minutes to respond to Blitz's question.

"Have you ever heard of Zhon Gnamhat?" Kurt asked.

Blitz turned, saying, "Quit mumbling."

"Zhon Gnamhat," Kurt repeated.

"Sounds like a bad cold, or straight out of Alice in Wonderland," Blitz laughed.

"As implausible as it sounds," Kurt continued, "Zhon is a very important location in China. It is, in fact, the main Red Chinese leadership compound. It has developed in importance as a think tank with communist leaders, as the years go by. It also happens to be located next door to the Forbidden City."

"So it is a suburb of Beijing," Blitz commented, adding, "that makes it easy, and also within our capabilities. Do you think we might catch some big Red Communists?"

"Very likely," Kurt replied. "We might even catch Chairman Hu," adding, "I would hate to fire our air-to-air missiles indiscriminately into the China countryside," chuckling. "We would be very likely to hurt some of the millions of China's newly evolved Christians," adding, "Hopefully they will now be able to lead China in a way never thought of. Never dreamed of in China's long history."

Blitz nodded, "Give me the new coordinates," adding, "American Christians should take note."

"In a minute," Kurt responded, nodding, and taking the correct maps out of a side case.

"Coordinates for ships One, Two and Number Three are first," Kurt reiterated. "They have to come first," as he then relayed the vital information to Blitz, and then onto air-to-air missiles, Number four, five, and six.

"Stand by Cheyenne Mountain. Sending three at ships One, Two and Three. Four minutes, forty-five seconds," Kurt announced.

Time stood still to Kurt as it seemed the whole world waited for, unknowingly, the crucial life saving three missiles, roaming space, to hit their mark.

"Three times three," the computer spat out. "Give those shooters a Kupee doll."

After a long two minute pause, Cheyenne then blared, "The three ships are gone, benefit of three direct hits. You were correct on the dud ship. It evidently still had nuclear missiles aboard. One of them must not have been properly contained, because your missile caused a nuclear blast," adding, "The coast of China will get it worse, but Japan, Malaysia, and the Philippines will also get big tidal waves. The rest of the nuclear missiles, if any, are resting harmlessly on the bottom of the sea."

Blitz and Kurt smiled at the good news, as Kurt gave Blitz the final computer adjustments and analysis, plus coordinates to lob the final three air-to-air missiles in, and around Beijing, the Forbidden City, and Zhon Gnamhat, only this time they were air-to ground missiles.

"I have recalculated our missiles," Kurt intoned, "to allow them to make the necessary ground swoop. Make sure you unlock the new attachment on your engage buttons," adding, "I have also refigured our fuel. We must send our missiles to those coordinates I have just set on our three remaining air-to-ground missiles. They must be fired as I count. Kurt looking at his watch, yelled, "Fire one."

Blitz dutifully pushed all the necessary activating buttons.

"Fire two," Kurt continued counting. "Fire three."

Kurt then told Blitz, "Make a beeline to the new landing site at these marks. We are almost out of fuel."

"Where is it?" Blitz asked.

"Okinawa," Kurt replied, "and we should run out of fuel half way down the runway."

"Okinawa," Blitz responded. "Of course. I should have thought of it."

"I have just sent a message to the island that we are coming," Kurt laughed. "Ready or not."

"The Forbidden City no longer exists," the Cheyenne Mountain run computer blared. "I hope that was the intention," adding, "Beijing and the China coast are also a complete mess."

Blitz and Kurt, feigning an imaginary toast, dropped the F-XXII to a lower altitude to help, should they have to glide into Okinawa. Kurt then noting, "Mr. Hu, as Christ clearly pointed out, 'Those who take the sword will perish by the sword,' Christ also pointed out, God could easily grant to those who have faith, 'Twelve legions of angels.'"

The F-XXII, was now in the final race of its life, as it nosed in to Okinawa's main north-south runway the gallant plane was in the hands of the Devine. Its fuel tanks were bone dry.

"God be with us," Kurt proclaimed, as Blitz, using all his piloting skills, kept the plane in a glide path as long as possible.

Kurt, excitedly, leapt up and down, in his buckled seat, as F-XXII's wheels touched down at the far south end of the runway, and then coasted unscathed, and unhindered, to the middle of the runway.

The plane sat in lonely silence, as Blitz and Kurt gave thanks, and each other the "V" sign.

Their attention was quickly diverted, however, to a growing noise emanating out of the north part of the island runway. Blitz, seeing the cause, proudly proclaimed, "Looks like God has sent one of his legions of angels, but in the form of a hundred," abruptly halting, "I mean," laughing, "in the form of a thousand United States American Marines," waving both arms vigorously, along with Kurt, as the enveloping Marines fully surrounded the spent F-XXII. These latter day angels filled the eardrums to the full with their cheers, and olive drab angel wings.

Printed in the United States
by Baker & Taylor Publisher Services

Printed in the United States
by Baker & Taylor Publisher Services